Jim Driver

was born in Yorkshire in 1954. He is a publisher, writes regularly for *Time Out* magazine, and in 1994 edited the highly-acclaimed *Rock Talk*. He lives in south London with a large number of books (quite a few with the same title), and is regularly chastised for not answering his front door.

Funny Talk

edited by
Jim Driver

The
Do-Not
Press

First Published in Great Britain in 1995 by
The Do-Not Press
PO Box 4215
London SE23 2QD

A Paperback Original

ISBN 1 899344 01 2

British Library Cataloguing in Publication Data. A catalogue record for
this book is available from the British Library.

Printed and bound in Great Britain by The Guernsey Press Co Ltd,
Guernsey, Channel Islands

Contents

Introduction ... **7**

Contributors ... **11**

1. *Mark Lamarr*: 'Narnia Revisited' (a true story) ... **15**

2. *Michael Palin* remembers 'Sid', the driver
from Hell ... **21**

3. *Hattie Hayridge* debunks some 'Myths Mrs'... **29**

4. *Alan King*: 'And His Amazing Flying Rabbits' ... **35**

5. A ride in the jalopy with *Max Bygraves* as he
remembers 'My First Car' ... **41**

6. *Bob Mills* says 'It's A Funny Old Game' ... **43**

7. *Jeremy Hardy* on 'Sex and Drugs and...?' ... **49**

8. There's 'No Accounting For Comedy'
with *Arnold Brown* ... **53**

9. *Jon Ronson* is 'Funny' ... **63**

10. 'A short address at the comedy college'
from *John Hegley* ... **70**

11. *Ronnie Golden* was an 'Evil Purveyor of Filth' ... **71**

12. *Peter Curran*: 'Five Years In A PC Camp' ... **75**

13. *Paul Whitehouse* is getting a little tired
of 'Questions' ... **81**

14. Viv Stanshall remembered by *Glen Colson* ... **85**

15. *Malcolm Hay* mourns Bill Hicks... **87**

16. *Jim Driver* on 'Sit-Coms' ... **93**

17. *Malcolm Hardee* reveals all about 'Freddie Mercury's Birthday Party' ... **123**

18. 'Laurel and Hardy' remembered by *Ralph McTell* ... **129**

19. 'The stand up comedian sits down' by *John Hegley* ... **136**

20. *Anita Chaudhuri* on 'Women In Comedy'... **137**

21. 'Litter' by *Norman Lovett* ... **143**

22. *Dwight Z Giannetti* on 'The Craft of Being Funny: Comedy and its Role in Western Culture During the Latter Part of the Twentieth Century. ... **147**

23. 'First Day at School': Will Hay ... **155**

24. *Mark Steel* on 'Fame'... **161**

25. *Richard Bucknall*: 'Agent Provocateur' ... **167**

26. *Bruce Dessau* writes about 'Writing About Comedy' ... **173**

27. *Hank Wangford* recalls a time when the cry (in Nashville, at least) was 'Gorbachov Is The Antichrist!'... **181**

New *Ray Lowry* cartoons on pages...
10, 28, 40, 48, 62, 80, 146, 160, 166, 180, 185

Introduction

First of all: sorry to Miles, who thought he was going to be doing this Introduction. So did I, but seeing as how the last contribution arrived on the day before the finished book had to be at the printers, sending him a finished proof proved impossible. Entering copy, organising the layout and writing the introduction sounds like a hard week's work, and it is. Not many people can have managed it all in a day. (Well, nineteen hours really, we cheated and started at midnight.) You can bet your last expense account lunch that this isn't how things are done at Penguin.

This is the second book from The Do-Not Press and the second in the ...*Talk* series. The next will concern itself with the subject of film, and should be published in the autumn of 1995. The reason I've yet not mentioned the title of this eagerly-awaited publication is because we can't seem to decide on one. Favourite so far is *Talkie Talk*. There seems to be a little opposition around the office to that, (can't see why) but I'll hopefully be able to bring them round in time.

Funny Talk was certainly an, *er...* 'challenge' to put together. Most agents (with the honourable exception of R Bucknall, Esq) are not exactly in favour of books like this, and not one potential contributor approached via their agent agreed to join in; most didn't even reply. Pure coincidence, I'm sure.

We lost a few potential contributors along the way for various reasons. The most reasonable excuses were 'writing my autobiography/novel/shopping list' (several), 'because you're a cringing bastard' (Spike Milligan) and 'dead' (Peter Cook and Viv Stanshall). Spike Milligan didn't really say that: it was a feeble attempt to inject a little humour in to this Introduction. But sadly, Peter Cook and Viv Stanshall really did die.

Thanks to all the living (and dead) contributors and to everyone who helped in any way at all. It's been appreciated.

Jim Driver

For Stephanie and Daniel

'This looks promising – they're looking for a stand-up comic for the light entertainment wing of the Bloomsbury group.'

The Contributors

This is intended purely as a short, largely adjective-free description of the Contributors. It goes without saying that they are all wonderful human beings and extremely talented artists.

Ray Lowry is one of the best-known cartoonists in Britain; his work appears regularly in *The Times*, *Mojo* and *Private Eye*. **Mark Lamarr** is a stand-up comedian, writer, and a TV & radio presenter. Monty Python founder **Michael Palin** is a writer (his début novel, *Hemingway's Chair* was recently published by Methuen and comes warmly recommended), TV presenter and traveller. **Hattie Hayridge** is a comedian, writer and plays the part of Holly, the computer in BBC TV's *Red Dwarf*. **Alan King** works as a music promoter and manager. **Max Bygraves** is a light entertainment legend. **Bob Mills** is a comedian and TV and radio presenter. **Jeremy Hardy** is a stand-up comedian, writer and radio presenter. **Arnold Brown** is a comedian who used to be an accountant. **Jon Ronson** is a *Guardian* columnist, writer and TV presenter.

John Hegley is a poet, comedian and writer. The poems here are taken from two of his Methuen books, *Can I Come Down Now Dad?* and *Five Sugars Please*. **Ronnie Golden** is a comedian, writer and musician who fronts the band Ronnie and the Rex. **Peter Curran** is a radio and TV presenter currently working on London's GLR. **Paul Whitehouse** is a comedian, writer and actor, often seen on TV in such programmes as the *The Fast Show* and Harry Enfield (it would only be fair to point out that his writing partner, Charles Higson, offered some assistance). **Glen Colson** sent a long fax with all his details on, but we lost it; from what we can remember, he has just finished work on the new Jerry (Lee?) Lewis CD and is chairman of Big Talk Communications. **Malcolm Hay** is a lecturer in drama and Comedy Editor for *Time Out* magazine. **Malcolm Hardee** is a manager, comedian and top dog at the Willesden Empire and Up The Creek comedy venues. **Ralph McTell** is a musician, singer/songwriter and radio & TV presenter. **Anita Chaudhuri** is Deputy Editor of *Time Out* magazine.

Norman Lovett is a comedian, writer and actor who was the original Holly in *Red Dwarf*. **Dwight Z Giannetti** is sometime Associate Professor of Comedy and Neuropsychology at the University of West Carolina. **Will Hay** is sadly dead. **Mark Steel** is a comedian, writer and radio presenter. **Richard Bucknall** is a comedy agent and runs RBM from London's Covent Garden. **Bruce Dessau** is a writer and journalist of some note; among his many books is (coincidentally) *The Official Red Dwarf Handbook*. **Hank Wangford** is a writer, radio & TV presenter, journalist and Country Music singer/songwriter who, in his spare time, dabbles in gynaecology.

Funny Talk

published in association with

1
Mark Lamarr

...'Narnia Revisited' – a true story

The Players
(in order of appearance)
Mark Lamarr – narrator.
Sean Lock – popular comedian.
Bill Bailey – popular comedian and half of the popular
comedy double act, The Rubber Bishops.
Simon Godley – popular comedian, one half of popular
comedy duo, The Nice People, and dentist.
Simon Munnery – popular comedian.
Jeff Green – popular comedian.
Ian Cognito – popular comedian.

The events in this story took place some years back, before TV took over my life, and death threats became commonplace. Barely a day goes by nowadays that I don't receive, say, some human excrement through my letterbox, together with a cut-and-paste Sex Pistols-cover-style-like letter, and the weekend doesn't begin properly until my Saturday morning horse's head in the bed wake-up call arrives.

The day in question, though, was an average day in the life of a jobbing comedian. I'd gone out, done a gig in a pub and was on my way to another when I thought I'd nip home to pick up a clean pair of jokes, brush up on my timing and check for any messages. So, after a quick wash and brush-up, I'm as clean as John The Baptist on a double-shift. The red light's flashing on my answering machine and I'm ready to go. Only one message: a dog growling. I save the message, figuring I can get a tenner for it from *That's Life*, and play it one more time. It's a dog talking this time, so I play it over and over until I can work out what it wants, and finally I realise it's saying 'dead man'. Then I play it over and over again to make sure it really says 'dead man', save it again so I can scare myself when I get home, and leave.

I have to get up early the next day, so when I get in at about 11.30pm, I play 'dead man' a few more times like you would play a new single until you get bored with it, then go to bed and read. As luck would have it, I was going through a phase of reading those true murder type books at the time, so to say that 'dead man' wasn't playing on my mind would be a self-delusion of Eubank proportions. But I'd calmed myself with the knowledge that I couldn't remember doing anything that warranted my death, and if I'd have wanted to put the shits up someone, I'd have opted for the long drawn out 'I know where you live 'number rather than the 'two word slam the phone down as if I were more scared than the target' routine.

It was just after midnight and I was discovering the facts behind the death of Lawrence Shead (skull smashed in with an electric iron) when the phone rang. It only rang once, but with the volume of Metallica encoring at Wembley, with the speed of a pickpocket working a marathon and with the intensity of an 'I'm having an affair' scene in *EastEnders*. I picked it up before the first ring was finished, but all I heard was the sound of it being put down at the other end. Apart from getting up to turn the light on (Hey Mr Murderer, I'm in this room!) I spent the next five minutes wondering whether it was possible for the human mind to invent a scarier scenario for itself, when the van pulled up outside and I had my answer.

It was a big white van, the type you'd transport guns and dead bodies in, and it sat outside my house, its engine running with all the menace of a big white van with its engine running. I wouldn't expect you to understand. Just as you wouldn't believe the fear induced by the sound of a big white van engine being turned off. Had I been sharing a flat with Quincy, I could confirm that I'm the only living person who's suffering from rigor mortis, suffice to say I was as stiff as Enoch Powell at a Public Enemy concert. Until my door buzzer rang, that is.

A word of explanation: my buzzer creates tidal waves that could cover China. If my buzzer went off in a forest and no one was there, I'd get calls from Paraguay asking me to turn it down. I can stand at my window watching someone touch my buzzer and I'll still jump a few feet in shock. This time, though, my buzzer sounded like Satan with a bad crack habit screaming through a megaphone down my aural canal. I picked up the handset before my ears had stopped ringing (three weeks before, in fact), whispered, 'Hello?', and heard a host of angels and their heavenly band reply: 'It's Sean, can you come down?' Okay, it was only Sean Lock, but in this particular circumstance, that's just as good. I ran downstairs and there stood Sean and Bill Bailey, either side of a huge wardrobe. I blurted out the whole story in a few seconds, and called to whoever was in the wardrobe to make themselves known or forever hold my fist in their mouth – which proved to be strangely fitting, as the inhabitant was my dentist, Simon Godley. They all apologised for making the second call (though not the first) and over a cup of tea explained their version of events.

Sean had been helping Bill move house and they decided to turn up at Simon's with the wardrobe 'he'd asked them for', actually convincing the Dentist that he'd forgotten, Simon reluctantly agreeing to accept, on condition that they could look him in the eye and swear that he'd asked them to deliver it. On production of the facts, he enjoyed the wind-up so much that he suggested me as next port of call. I enjoyed it so much I suggested Simon Munnery as the next port of call. Stopping only to make the obligatory non-speaking phone call, we loaded up the wardrobe and set off for the home of the Urban Warrior.

Munnery only lived a few minutes away, so we were still in high spirits when we unloaded the wardrobe at Urban Warrior Villas. Bill and the Dentist entered the wardrobe while Sean and I put on our wind-up caps. Luckily 'Gullibility' is Simon's middle name – at least that's what he's been told – so it didn't take long to convince him that he'd asked for the wardrobe. But 'Politeness' is his other middle name and he was trying to explain that he didn't think he would get it up his stairs, when Sean went for it. Maybe it was my near-death experience that prevented me from going for it, after all thus far only I had suffered closet-rophobia – or whatever the word is for furniture-fear – but it was a joy to watch Sean's artlessness matched by Simon's guilelessness.

'Why don't you see how big it is inside,' was all it took for the Urban Warrior to approach Pandora's Nightmare. A simple 'boo' from the emergent Dentist and Bishop was all that was needed to reduce a once relatively proud man to a respiratory wreck. Munnery enjoyed the wind-up so much he suggested Jeff Green as next port of call.

Jeff lived about 15 minutes away from Munnery's, but only yards away from Godley's dental practice, so the Dentist decided it may be a professional step backwards to be be caught by one of his patients at 1.30am indulging in cupboard-shifting shenanigans, and prudently stayed in the van for this particular episode, thus missing out on all the fun of lugging the devilish box to the first-floor flat.

We made so much noise banging the wardrobe against the stairs, hand-rail, walls and whatever else we could find to bang it against, that it was difficult to drown it out with our giggling and whisper-shouting of 'shhh' and 'sssh'. We only managed to wake one other tenant but, unluckily, she seemed to possess a unique mixture of Mr Bean-like nervousness and fiery Mediterranean passion, simultaneously filling us with compassion and dread as she repeatedly cried, 'What's happening?' Finally we positioned the gag machine at Jeff's front door, a few of us got inside, a few others rang the bell, and the prankster quartet waited. And waited. And finally realised he wasn't in. By which point our downstairs inquisitor our had changed her tune to 'I'm calling the police', followed by the very convincing sound of, well, her calling the police. I bet Freud's *Studies On Hysteria* could comfortably explain why we panicked – if only we'd had time to read it – because to this day I don't understand what we thought we'd done wrong when we performed one of those Scooby Doo-type 'Oooh, let's get out of here'-s. Down the stairs, in to the van, off home. Evening over.

Meanwhile, Jeff had been in Chester for a week having some kind of Tears Of A Clown/Mid-Twenties Crisis/Generally Pissed Off-type trauma, so when he returned a few days later to find he'd completely forgotten an important gig *and* that his lodger had accidentally erased all his answering machine messages, he was in no mood to have his entrance blocked. Pausing only to flick through his trusty Longfellow anthology to find a suitable phrase, and settling for the classic 'move the fucking wardrobe now', he dashed off a notelet and posted it through his neighbour's letterbox.

A few days later, Jeff was holding his monthly bridge and sherry morning when another comedian – who should remain anonymous, but instead chooses to call himself Ian Cognito – espied the object of delight, consulted Longfellow and said: 'I can get £30 for that' before loading it up and doing a daylight flit.

That week Cognito was performing at a new club which encouraged experimentation around a tired old stand-up format. Never one to turn his back on any kind of experimen-

tation, our hero set up the wardrobe on stage, got in and
worked around the simple premise that this was the club's
dressing-room. Throughout the evening the compère would
periodically open the double doors and our man would be
changing or brushing his teeth. The climax of the evening
approached, it was time for the star turn to make his simultane-
ous entrance and exit, the double doors were disengaged and
the lucky punters were treated to the unforgettable sight of a
grown man furiously masturbating in a wardrobe.

After this, the whereabouts of the wardrobe are a complete mystery – to me at least – but I beg of you, if you ever
find any type of furniture at a phone box with my number in its
hand, please alert the local constabulary. Approach with caution: it is shelved and dangerous.

2
Michael Palin
...on 'Sid'

There is no getting away from Monty Python. I don't just mean people shouting 'Welease Wodger!' across a crowded pub, or letters from earnest Americans wanting to know more about blancmanges or Japanese students claiming to have learned their English from *The Matching Tie and Handkerchief Album*, or John Cleese wanting to borrow money. I mean there is no getting away from the people we created.

Perhaps, in those heady days of the late '60s, when The Beatles had just broken up and Monty Python had just come together we did genuinely believe that, like the Goons we so admired (well, *I* so admired, anyway), we were creating a whole new gallery of fictional characters. Mr Gumby, Mrs Niggerbaiter, Ethel the Frog, Doug and Dinsdale Piranha and others sprang, it seemed, from deep inside our tormented imaginations in two or three concentrated years of collective creativity. It was all, somehow, 'new'. Even nowadays, 26 years on, there is much talk of the barriers we broke down, the lines we crossed and the unmatched originality of our work.

But, of course, Monty Python's characters were far from original. They could be traced directly to the schoolmasters, vicars, television personalities, window cleaners, barmen, characters in war films, and even occasionally women whom we had all encountered at some time in our middle-class English provincial childhoods. We might put them in different contexts – vicars in a wrestling ring, cricketers in a Pasolini film, tight-lipped explorers climbing the Uxbridge Road – but nearly all our characters had their living embodiments somewhere.

Over the last two and a half decades, a lot of those living embodiments have come back to haunt us. You find yourself squeezed on the Manchester shuttle next to some one who says 'Nudge, nudge. Know what I mean?' and isn't Eric Idle. There *are* chartered accountants who want to become lion tamers and some dangerous criminals *do* think that their teeth move around in their heads. Silly documentary titles we were once so pleased with, like *Is The Queen Sane?* are probably being discussed at the very highest levels of the BBC at this very moment. You may take a wonderful, wild, whacky, irreverent look at the world but you can be sure that, when you least expect it, the wonderful, wild, whacky irreverent world will almost certainly come back and give you a good kick up the backside.

Take Sid. Please.

Sid was one of the two drivers entrusted with carrying the Python team around the country during our one and only stage tour of Britain, which we had, whackily and irreverently, called The First Farewell Tour. It was the early summer of 1973. We wore long hair and flares (except for John, who has never allowed his wardrobe to be dictated by the whim of fashion. I swear he's worn the same pair of trousers ever since I've known him). In less than four years we had churned out 40 television shows, three albums, two books and a full-length feature film, *And Now For Something Completely Different*. We were hot. In fact we were very hot. And three of us – Neil Innes, Terry Jones and myself – were in the back of a car with no air-conditioning, driven by a chauffeur with no sense of direction. A character we had, unaccountably, never thought of inventing. Well, now we didn't need to invent him. He was here, sitting in front of us. He was small, elderly, myopic and driving us aimlessly around the sterile approach roads to Birmingham in a Queen Mother of a Daimler. His name was Sid, and he was a Python character long before Python.

A few nights earlier the tour had opened, fairly disastrously, at the Gaumont Theatre, Southampton. All the sound cues, music, on-screen film inserts and our radio mikes were the sole responsibility of one engineer, Dave. He was, quite predictably, falling apart. He had not slept for a week and was kept going only by fear. The results were alarming and unpredictable. Film would come up without sound, music cues would spring out loud and clear in the middle of sketches, only to be hastily strangled. Worst of all, despite several days of rehearsal, Dave was having serious trouble remembering our names. He would see two characters on stage and raise the mikes hopefully on what, to his over-amphetamined perceptions, appeared to be a two-hander between Eric and Graham Chapman. In fact, as once happened, it was Eric and myself on stage while the late, great Dr Chapman, mike raised to the full by Dave, sat on the lavatory backstage, complaining to the entire auditorium about the fucking awful audience.

Graham drank heavily in those days and was using the booze to cope with the extra stress and strain of the tour. This was, of course, hopeless. It is clearly possible to bang drums, run your fingers along a keyboard or even play legendary guitar solos while unable to walk along a white line, but I've rarely seen anyone's comedy timing improved by the bottle. Graham would often come on stage late or leave the stage early, leaving the other actors to improvise as best they could. One memorable night, in Cardiff, he forgot to come on at all. I was sat on stage as Ken Shabby, a cheerfully revolting character whose job it was to clean out public toilets – *'Is there promotion involved? Oh yeah! After five years they give me a brush'*. Beside me on the

sofa was Connie Booth, for whose hand in marriage I was waiting to ask her very English upper-crust father. The sketch could
not begin without Graham as the father, for he had the opening
line. All I could do was paw Connie and clear my throat dis-
gustingly and gob on the carpet as we awaited his arrival. After
about one-and-a-half minutes of gobbing and throat-clearing
there was still no sign of Graham and John Cleese, waiting in
the wings dressed as a Bishop for the next sketch, came on in
desperation and did Graham's lines, as best he could. We were
all furious with Graham but the sketch never went as well
again.

Anyway, the pressure of the tour was increasing and
Sid's inability to find the centre of Birmingham, or indeed anywhere, led some of us to travel any long or complicated distance by train, or hired car in order to avoid the great Daimler.
But it was not possible to avoid it altogether.

A few days later we found ourselves in Edinburgh. The
distance from the theatre to the Post House Hotel was about
two miles. Ten minutes' drive at most, along the main Glasgow
road. After two hectic shows in one afternoon we flung ourselves gratefully into the back of the Daimler and Sid set out for
the hotel. After 25 minutes we looked out on a bleak and deso-
late expanse of moorland, with the lights of Edinburgh far
behind us. A sign flashed by in the gloom. 'Peebles', it read.

'Is this the Glasgow Road, Sid?' one of us asked.

'I think so,' said Sid.

'It said Peebles.'

'Where did it say Peebles?' asked Sid with interest.

'On that road sign, Sid. On the sign on the side of the
road, Sid.'

Sid took this information in with only mild interest.

'Turning just coming up,' he said authoritatively.
Moments later we found ourselves in a narrow, dimly-lit track
amidst the bleak grey pebble-dash of a new housing estate. Sid,

ever-hopeful that this might be the link road between Scotland's two great cities, drove along until he came to a brick wall. Only then did Sid accept that this was not the Glasgow road. It was a cul-de-sac.

After the shows at the King's Head Theatre Glasgow, it was no better. A two-minute drive to the Albany Hotel, a journey almost impossible to cock up, took Sid nearly half-an-hour.

'I was confused by all the lights,' he complained bitterly. As Glasgow on a Sunday night was not, in those days, exactly Piccadilly Circus, we could only conclude that the lights he was referring to must have been traffic lights. Sid was now so consistently wrong that, as Neil Innes observed, 'He makes a mockery of the law of averages.' A sort of compulsive fascination kept us loyal to Sid's Daimler, until one morning we left the Leeds-Bradford Post House to travel back to London. At the top of the drive we came to a fast, straight, main road. Two large signs faced us. One said 'North' and the other 'South'.

Sid turned North.

For the final leg of the tour Terry Jones and I chose to travel in the other car. This was driven by a man named Bill. Bill was of a similar age to Sid, but a bigger, much more confident man. However, Bill insisted that we travel in convoy, with Sid, John and Eric in front (Graham had his own personal chauffeur, a handsome young man, constantly pulling into lay-bys, where the occupants of the car would enjoy stiff gin and tonics). The idea of Bill following Sid seemed a prime example of an out of the frying pan into the fire situation, but Bill shouted over his shoulder that there was a reason for it. Sid's car wasn't working very well. The brakes were in a very dangerous state. It would have been nice to have been able to catch Sid up and warn his occupants of this, but Sid was touching 100mph by then and Bill couldn't get near him.

Heavy rain hit us a few miles from Bristol. Visibility was atrocious. Our windows were steaming up alarmingly.

Occasionally we could catch a glimpse of Sid's Daimler through the murk. It was swaying about like a raft in storm. Terry, now thoroughly alarmed by the ratio of velocity to visibility, suggested Bill might like to clear the windscreen so he could see out. 'It's just the rain. Nothing we can do about it,' Bill assured him.

'It's mist. It's on the inside,' Terry persisted.

'Can't do anything about that,' said Bill, cheerfully.

'Couldn't you use the de-mister?' Terry asked, as condensation slowly entombed us.

Bill looked quite impressed at this.

'Where's that then?'

Terry pointed to a knob on the dashboard marked 'De-mister'. Bill touched it warily and sure enough, after a moment or two the windscreen began to clear. Bill shook his head in awed disbelief.

The Kamikaze Brothers finally got us to Bristol and there, much to our relief, stood the ten-storey bulk of the Dragonara Hotel. For some reason, ahead of us, Sid had pulled up at the curve. He dismounted from the Daimler and was standing in the road looking to left and right.

'Everything all right, Sid?'

'I'm looking for someone to ask where the bloody hotel is.'

With one voice we all cried and pointed.

'It's there, Sid. It's there! Look! Across the roundabout at the bottom of the hill. It says "Dragonara" in enormous letters!'

With a reproachful look as if to say, 'You just put that sign there didn't you?' Sid climbed back into the Daimler and we progressed down the hill towards the hotel. At the bottom of the hill, almost unbelievably, Sid turned left, away from the hotel, over a low hill, in the direction of the docks.

At this point, those of us lucky enough to be in Bill's vehicle fell back into our soft leather seats, hollering and hollering with mirth, disbelief and the satisfaction of knowing that, for once, we would get first choice of rooms.

We were close enough to the Dragonara Hotel to see the lights of the foyer when Bill swung away to the left and followed Sid towards the docks.

People often ask if there is any subject that we wonderful, wild, whacky, irreverent comedy mould-breakers would never tackle. The only one I can think of is chauffeurs.

Smorgasm...

3
Hattie Hayridge
...'Myths Mrs'

There have been myths built up about comedy ever since a Neanderthal quipped the first well-timed 'Ug'. Take, for example, the well-known heckle put-down line 'I remember my first drink'. Well, I'd say that most comics don't. I guess mine would have been at about the age of three, a sneaky sip from my mum's Guinness while she was doing the dusting, but I couldn't swear to it. I think there are a good many myths that could be dispelled.

The myth that modern comics are all middle-class with fake working-class accents...

Every July, along the section of the A-road we called our home town, there would be a carnival. Obviously, since I was brought up on the London/Hertfordshire border, and not in Rio, this meant a Saturday afternoon parade of lorry-loads of happy, smiling people from the Rotary Club, Barclays Bank and the Gas Board. They would be interspersed with the Dagenham Girl Pipers and beauty queens from the surrounding area showing off the regal wave they'd borrowed for the occasion. A murmur could sometimes be detected among the expectant throng: 'Aw, she's come all the way from Harlow!' It was the highlight of the social calendar and people would come out to crowd on the pavement and watch the procession pass by. Innocent, warm, trusting days, when no traffic would be allowed along the High Street, and no one expected to be served in a shop until the carnival was over.

The year I was nine, the local newspaper decided to send out Mr Mercury, a mystery man in a mac who would mingle with the waiting crowds. His mission, which he'd obviously decided to accept, was to search out punters waving that week's issue of the paper, ask them a simple question, and then give them a fiver if they got it right. My best friend Jane and I were thrilled therefore to be approached by a dodgy man in a trilby, who separately took us down the side of the pub and asked us the name of the statue at the top of the road. We both knew the answer, the Eleanor Cross, and each won our £5. Innocent, warm, trusting days, when a nine year-old could wander up an alley with a stranger, come back with a fiver, and nobody thought any more of it. Anyway, he wrote down our names and our reaction to being two of the lucky winners. At the time I could have sworn I'd said, 'Blimey, I didn't fink I'd win nothing', which was translated into print as 'It's wonderful, I never dreamed I'd be so lucky'

Since then, I've had various 'awfully', 'dreadfully' and 'frightfully'-s thoughtfully added to my vocabulary by journalists to save me from meself guv'nor. Lawks a lummee.

The Myth that comics lie about their childhood – or, it's all in the delivery…

I was an only child. I still am. My parents had been married 17 years before they had me. They used to have a cocker spaniel. It took them a while to adjust. Happy days, though, crawling through the park with a stick in my mouth. I was indeed my parents' first and only child, born when they were both in their mid-forties. My mother had gone to the doctor telling him that she thought she was pregnant, and he'd replied 'Don't be so stupid, not at your age.' So, since they were brought up to believe expert opinion and to respect authority, they knew the doctor must be right. She carried on with her cleaning job at the Coach and Horses, and going to her ballroom dancing club. Six months later, my mother couldn't sleep one night because of the pains in her stomach (sort of) area. On his way to work in the morning, my dad stopped by at the phone box and rang the doctor, saying that perhaps my mum had appendicitis. The doctor said he'd try and get round after morning surgery, and my dad carried on to the nursery where he worked growing cucumbers. The doctor turned up around lunch-time, my mum opened the door, so he knew it couldn't be that serious, and he examined her. 'I've got to get a second opinion, but I think you're having contractions.' Still not entirely sure what was wrong with her, my mother was rushed into hospital, and gave birth to a 4lb baby girl. My dad, meanwhile, having been told that my mum had been taken away in the ambulance, arrived there from work to be shown me. Both parents lived the rest of their lives in a state of shock. My parents never told me where I came from, they just kept asking me.

The Myth That Heckling is Harmless Fun...

The first night I went to a comedy club was because the film we wanted to see was full up. My friend and I sat right down the front, because strangely enough, there were empty seats right down the front. We sat near a couple, who looked as if they were on their first date together. The bloke could have come straight from the statement enquiries counter and was out to make an impression. He also seemed to be on his first heckle. 'Shut up,' he tried. This stopped the comic in his tracks, since he'd not heard such a pathetic heckle in a very long time. 'You shut up,' he replied. Obviously stumped now, the bloke left it a while before he came back with a confident nod to his date and, 'Go on, shut up'. The comic drastically upped the stakes with 'Piss off, you sad wanker' to which Bank Man grabbed his glass and hurled his beer over the comic. The comic hurled his beer over the punter who was by now on his feet and desperate to save his rapidly diminishing chances of a second date. He grabbed the bottom of the mic-stand. The comic grabbed the top half, with a 'Let go, you wanker!' But Wanker wouldn't let go, and the mic-stand was pulled backwards and forwards in true heave-ho fashion. Finally, the comic said, 'Well if you want it so bad, you can fucking have it,' and let go. Wanker pulled the mic-stand straight back, smack into his girlfriend's face. I'll leave the rest of the scene to Michael Winner's imagination.

The Myth That Comics Have No Dress-Sense…

My first day at *Red Dwarf* rehearsals started in London at 10am on a Sunday morning, immediately after the last night of the Edinburgh Festival – in Edinburgh. The *Red Dwarf* producers had arranged for me to catch the 7am plane back to London, where a speeding car would whisk me straight to the studio for 10am. Saturday night was party night in Edinburgh, but because the next day was so important, I decided I'd only stay about an hour. I left the party, arrived back at the rented flat to find I hadn't taken my keys. I went back to the party to find that the person I was sharing with had by this time got off and gone off with somebody. I went back to the flat to see if they'd gone there, then back to the party, then back to the flat, and spent the whole night in this particular rut. At 6am I was slumped on the steps outside the flat, as the taxi came to take me to the airport. That is how I came to arrive at rehearsals the Sunday morning – where trainers, jeans and T shirt was the norm – wearing high heels, laddered tights, the remains of last night's make-up and a blue frilly '50s cocktail dress.

Myth: Heckling is Harmless Fun II. Director's Cut

Malcolm Hardee's Tunnel Club was a notorious venue. It was the rowdiest, roughest and most exciting club on the circuit. Nestling between the south entrance to the Blackwall Tunnel and an industrial estate, the smell of the Tate and Lyle sugar factory outside could only be matched by the smell of frightened performer on the inside. The atmosphere was like the wild west, not just on the stage but hanging on to a bucking bronco and seeing how long you could stay on for.

I was on stage when a bloke walked out from the toilets, walked across the back of the stage, stood behind me and lifted my dress up over my head. Well, I don't know if it was the shock, or the embarrassment of having sensible knickers on or what, but I landed him a well-aimed kick and carried on kicking him all the way back to his seat. I then went back to the mic in a hot flurry and carried on with my act. After a couple of minutes, during which time this same bloke must have been rifling through his shopping, something which felt like a cricket-ball (and turned out to be an egg) hit me in the face. Either it numbed the nerve endings to my ears, or everything had gone silent. I walked over to where the man sat, lifted up a tray full of glasses, and held it a few inches above him. Thoughts rushed through my head as to whether a tray of broken glasses were about to rush through his. I decided 'maybe not'; walked back to the mic, said, 'Thank you and good night,' and got off.

Malcolm wandered back on stage, and gallantly asked the audience, 'Who thinks we should chuck this bloke out?' 'Yes', went up one cry, followed by yells of 'out of order' and 'bang out of order', and a posse was formed who grabbed the bloke and dragged him out through the mob. And hanged him from the nearest tree. No, that last bit's not true, but he did get a few pints over his head and I managed to land him a girly punch on his way past and out the door. Well that's that over, I thought, as my right eye started to swell. But I was laughing on the wrong side of my face. Malcolm re-introduced me on to the stage to carry on with the act. A few one-liners later, with my eye closing rapidly. I said, 'I'm getting off now I feel a bit dizzy.'

'What did you get off for?' asked a bloke at the bar, 'you were doing really well.'

'I dunno,' I had to reply, 'stupid really.'

I've since learned that trying to get an insurance policy guarding against members of the audience chucking stuff at you is the surest way of getting rid of insurance salesmen.

The myth of the difference between British and American comedy...

The first time I was on the New York subway, this bloke jumped on and called out: 'Is this going to 42nd Street?' No one answered, which the bloke wasn't slow to notice. 'Just because I'm black, none of you white motherfuckers are going to answer me, is that right?' No one answered...

Pause.

'Well I didn't answer,' I piped up, 'because I'm lost and I don' t know where it's going'.

'Hey lady!' he screamed, 'where did you get that accent?'

'England.'

'You from England? Wow that's funny.' He got off at the next stop... 'I like you, lady,' he laughed. Then shouted: 'But I still hate the rest of you motherfuckers!'

Most importantly, regarding the myth that comics just laze around all day watching telly...

Most comics work all day, going over and over their act, perfecting and honing their writing down to the

4
Alan King
...'And His Amazing Flying Rabbits'

It was the summer of 1986 when I had my first brush with the comedy scene. Before that, the funniest thing I'd seen was a grotty punk I'd spied in Greenwich market, wearing tartan trousers and a studded leather jacket with the immortal words 'Debussy' and 'Vaughan Williams' spelled out on the back. This incident had inspired me to go home and paint the words 'Various Groups' on my own biker jacket. *The Young Ones* had passed me by and on the few occasions I'd seen the *Comic Strip Presents…* it had left me cold.

It was a Sunday night and I was in search of a late drink, when I saw Winston's Wine Bar in Deptford. I nearly balked at the 50p admission price, but noticed some people at the bar I recognised. The crowd was a mixture of post New Romantic types and local south Londoners. The acts were all nondescript cabaret turns, not showbiz, but Brechtian art-school types, apart from one man with a thick north-eastern accent. He was either a genius or an imbecile: he balanced a carrot on a stick, sang *Fly Me to the Moon* and repeatedly told the audience that his name was Vic Reeves, 'top north-eastern comedian and singer'.

Maybe it was an empathy with the accent but I made the fateful decision that he was a comic genius, destined for the top, drop everything, sign him up and get involved. Vic was playing again the next night, Monday, at the Parrot Café in New Cross. He sat there with no trousers, a long-haired black wig and a girl on his knee. He again told the assembled throng that he was a top north-eastern comedian and singer. Brilliant or what?

Next day I went round his house and was astounded to find that Vic was an artist of rare distinction, with paintings even funnier than his act. He thrust a few copies of a magazine called *Viz* at me, and again I Saw The Light. This was better than anything off the telly. I think it was *Tina's Tits* that clinched it.

Back in the pub at Camberwell Grove I told my old schoolmate Bob about this great club that was opening. The regular night at Winston's had finished by this time, and its replacement, Vic Reeves' Variety Palladium, was about to start its six-week run. I knew that Bob used to frequent the comedy clubs, and I tried to get him to come and see the show. The Variety Palladium was a forerunner to the Big Night Out, with a regular cast of characters – misfits all – the brilliant John Houston Irvine, Paul Kennedy (now guitarist with top indie band Salad), Fred Aylward (who later metamorphosed into the Les character) and myself, having hastily cobbled together an act called Dr King and his Amazing Flying Rabbits. My act consisted of whirling cuddly toys around my head on bits of string, while telling stolen gags.

All this would mean nothing if it wasn't for the presence of one Rod Cooper. He was the single most hilarious thing that I will ever see, and every time he appeared I would literally piss myself with laughter. He would turn up infrequently and perform impromptu improvised spots, and then disappear into the night. If you knew Rod was going to be there, then it was worth bringing a change of pants. Where is he now?

Sadly, Bob never made it to the Palladium, but he did manage to attend the second Big Night Out. By November 1986 the show had transformed itself and transferred to Thursday nights at the Goldsmith's Tavern. It didn't start until 11pm, and there was a 3am bar. I don't think Bob had seen anything quite like it. An act called Tappy Lappy soon established itself as a crowd favourite, and by the next week Bob was performing a double act with me. The act consisted of little more than buying about ten pints of beer before going on stage, and throwing them over each other for approximately a minute-and-a-half, while simultaneously trying to fit in as many one-liners as possible. It was great fun and always left the stage knee-deep in props and spillage, much to the chagrin of Reeves.

By 1988 the Big Night had transferred to Saturday and – despite a £1 admission, but with the same 3am bar – it became hugely popular. Then disaster struck: violence erupted on three consecutive weeks, which temporarily put a stop to the antics.

A proper venue, The Albany Empire in Deptford, was chosen for a weekly run, and the momentum gathered. It soon sold out every week and rapidly became one of the hottest tickets in town. I remember once seeing Michael Grade and Alan Yentob present, along with Jools Holland, Glenn Tilbrook and Jonathan Ross.

Vic's Thursdays were taken up compèring at the Rub-A-Dub Club in Sydenham, which was a more traditional comedy club, featuring regular circuit acts. Vic soon established his own following and I can remember an irate Punt and Dennis storming home early because the compère was getting all the laughs. Inevitably, Vic started to do more and more TV work – including *01 For London* and *The Late Show* – and on these occasions I would fill in for him at the Rub-a-Dub, much to the audiences' disappointment.

It was around this time that I noticed that I was gradually being frozen out. Whereas at the Goldsmith's I'd normally done two or three spots a night, with Bob or solo, now Bob was working as a double act with Vic, and I was down to doing fillers. Although we did team up for The Three Scrutineers, an audience favourite and a highspot of the shows that never transferred to TV, along with Dr Heinz Mindpeeler, Mr Mysterious, Mr Membry Remembry Man and Les Pantellons. It didn't really bother me as I'd only started performing to fill the gaps, but I gradually stopped socialising with them as well. From being three or four blokes writing new material down the pub, it had become a large social group of hangers-on. Any material that had gone down well with the TV pundits was being repeated regularly and girlfriends were egging them on to be seen in the right places.

Maybe it was because I wasn't very funny, or very good; or because I had a propensity to drink vast amounts of alcohol (before, during and after the show); or maybe it was because I never had a script, took too much speed or had a few run-ins with the law; but as time went on, I was being left out in the cold. My dislike of the media brats didn't help, although Vic and Bob actively courted them.

Things got serious when Bob gave up his day-job, and Vic was put on a retainer by Channel 4. Next it was the big TV pilot show, which neither of them had the courage to tell me they were filming. It was left to Fred to come round two days before with an invitation. In the pub beforehand Paul White-house asked me why he was doing my parts. I got pissed, spilt some beer over some 'important people' and that was about the last time I bothered with them again.

In the summer of 1990 I started a brief run at the Paradise Bar, New Cross; it was a mixture of music and comedy and once again it was fuelled by increasing amounts of alcohol abuse. The music started taking over and on reflection I think it was just an excuse to be loud, aggressive, arrogant and pissed. It was probably a two-fingered salute to The Big Night Out.

I haven't really been to a comedy club since, save for one John Shuttleworth gig, and I doubt I will again. Despite everything it was probably the best time of my life. At least I got to tell Paul Gascoigne that it would be a good idea to go on *Gilbert's Fridge* (my fave TV show). I got to get pissed with Phil Cornwell, got to spill beer over some media brats and even cleared the hospitality suite of a television show by referring to our heroes as various parts of the female anatomy, thus leaving all the free drink for me.

Back in 1989 I'd called round to see Vic at home, it had started raining and he lent me a jacket. It was a leather jacket with studs on the back spelling out those immortal words 'Debussy' and 'Vaughan Williams'.

Rod Cooper, where are you now?

'It says here it's a wacky, structuralist sit-com set in a typical postmodern family,
written by Michael Ignatieff...'

5
Max Bygraves
...'My First Car'

I'll never forget my first car. The dealer – Sam Wheeler – told me it had had only one owner, a preacher. I think it must have been John the Baptist. I'll never forget my children running alongside it on the first outing gleefully shouting, 'It goes, it goes!'

My wife packed sandwiches, also a large picnic hamper and said, 'Let's visit our friends, the Hendersons.' This we did – it wasn't a long journey, they lived next door.

We always knew where the car was, we just followed the oil leak. When I bought it, there were two house-bricks on the passenger seat – I threw them out of the window. Sam Wheeler said, 'There goes your handbrake!' For two days I remained the owner, then I traded it in for a small saloon, a Ford Anglia, nearly new. I travelled up and down the UK on dates that were as far apart as Newcastle to Plymouth – it never left me down. At 38,000 miles I had a reconditioned engine fitted for £19 and notched up another 30,000 miles. It cost me £495 from a dealership in Edgware Road. The licence plate was GUF 650. I kept it for five years then sold it for £250 to a midget who was with an act known as The Shorts. He married a stripper. He put blocks on the pedals and ran it for seven more years, then sold it for £200.

I have had ten Rolls-Royces since 1954. I've never been without one. I also own a Daimler that was custom-built for King George VI in 1950. I had it brought back to its original state, but because of space needed, I will put it up for sale later this year. It will sadden me to see it go.

No car since has ever given me the fun I had in 'Guff', the Anglia.

6
Bob Mills

....after a lot of thought, decides 'It's a Funny Old Game.'

So, just two hours to write this article for 'Funny Talk'. I'm in a hotel room in Glasgow, just had a shower and a shave, got a table booked in the restaurant downstairs for nine o'clock. Having dinner with some people off the show. Sid Little, Eddie Large, Lionel Blair, The Krankies, and a few others.

Anyway...

It started about seven years ago, I'm working for The American Car Wash Co in King's Cross. Inside and out, £6.50; Engine Steaming, £12; Full Valet, £30-£50' extra for four-wheel drive.

Jan and I get a babysitter, set off to see a film, arrive at the cinema late, wind up at the Market Tavern instead. The Meccano Club's downstairs, so we pay our £1.50 and go in. Now, we've never been here before, we don't know if it's live music, theatre, disco or what. But there's a bar, and some atmosphere, so we give it a go. The lights go down, a bloke starts talking, and two and a half hours later, my life is irrevocably changed. The line-up that night was: Nickelodeon (a performance art double act), Eddie Zibbin (who reverted to Pat Condell and grew bitter, without enough people realising what a great comic he is), and a couple of brilliant, sharp, stand ups, Mark Thomas, and an indecently young-looking Kevin Day.

It was comedy.

But not like comedy I was used to. No Irishmen. No blokes walking into pubs. No nuns – actually, I think Kev did feature nuns rather heavily in his set, but you know what I mean, they weren't t buying drinks, or being raped.

So that's what happened. At the start of the evening I was a car washer who wanted to be a better paid car washer, maybe even a self-employed car washer. At the end of the evening, I'm a car washer who wants to be a stand-up comedian.

Kim Kinnie has just rung from the studio. He wants me to book a bigger table. Nicholas Parsons and Faith Brown have flown up early for tomorrow's show, and are coming to dinner.

Anyway...

I mope around for a few weeks, until Jan sees an advert for a comedy workshop at Jackson's Lane, and I sign up. Tony Allen, Kit Hollerbach, and Ivor Dembina run the classes and Mike Hayley and Hattie Hayridge are amongst the aspirants. I do a gig at the Lane, Tony Allen takes me to the Comedy Store, I do a gig there. Suddenly I'm a car-washing comic. A couple of years go by. I gig, I wash cars. I travel to Blackburn and back on a Rapide coach with Jo Brand for fifty quid, I polish a Volkswagen back to showroom condition for thirty quid. I go on tour with Arthur Smith and Nick Hancock in the back of a van, and think about asking the promoter for more money if I steam-clean the engine between shows. Then I do some TV and then I don't wash cars any more.

Somewhere in the midst of all this, I develop a style. Learn some stuff about performing, and become a half decent comic.

I play the Comedy Store and Jongleurs most weekends, as well as all the other venues. I do college tours, I work with all the people in the 'new wave' of comedy. I love and respect most of them, most of them love and respect me. I don't think too much about it, but something is bothering me.

I don't feel like an alternative comedian. *City Limits* hates me. *Time Out* only tolerate me because I'm too popular to openly slag off. I'm not racist, I'm not sexist, but I'm not getting asked on to Red Wedge Tours.

So I give the matter some thought. And this is what I think: When this whole movement started, back in the early eighties at the original Comedy Store, a group of performers appeared, they were mainly from universities and art colleges. They were from predominantly middle-class backgrounds. Their comedy was fresh, innovative, dangerous. They included in their ranks performers who would become some of the most important and influential entertainers of the generation, and a handful of them will undoubtedly leave their mark on the world of comedy for many years to come.

But they had a problem.

They were professional entertainers. Comedians.

In the eyes of the world, of their families and friends, they were in the same game as Jimmy Tarbuck, Max Bygraves and Little and Large.

Obviously this was not the image that they wanted to convey, so they invented – with the help of tho media – a whole new class of artist. The Alternative Comedian. Not merely laughter-makers, but revolutionaries, shapers of thought, polit-ical agitators. In order for this conceit to be valid, they had to create an enemy: adversaries who threatened to corrupt and pervert society. Racists, sexists, ageists. Fascists.

This role fell to the mainstream comics, in their suits and ties, with their prime time game shows, their Irishmen, their Mothers-in-Law, and their Nuns.

It all got out of hand.

It became Us and Them. I appeared on the Tarbuck show at the same time as I was regular compere at the Store. I did the same material, got a great response, but the following weekend two of my colleagues in the dressing room refused to speak to me. No names no pack drill, but to this day I'm rarely found drinking in the company of Mark Steel or Jeremy Hardy.

Fortunately, I now see a lot of comics who realise that it's all nonsense, Ben Elton is a great comic, Mark Thomas is a great comic, but nobody ever voted Labour because of them. Cannon and Ball are a great act. So are Roy Brown and Manning. They don't change opinions. They make people laugh.

I felt a whole lot happier once I'd realised that it didn't matter whether I felt like an alternative comedian or not, because no such animal actually existed.

So, how come I'm dining with The Krankies?
Television.

My first experience of TV was exquisitely painful. I was invited on to *Saturday Night Live*, hosted by the great Ben Elton and featuring the very best new comics of the day. I was very inexperienced. Tony Morewood, who had been around a while, advised me that the problem with telly was that once you had performed material on it, you couldn't do it live any more. I was terrified. I only had twenty minutes' worth of stuff. If I did seven minutes of it on the show, what was I going to do at live gigs?

Simple.

Write new material, and perform it on live network TV... for the first time.

I died on my arse.

Obviously.

Anyway, I recovered. Did some more telly, and the next thing you know, I've got my own game show: *Win Lose or*

Draw. Network slot, nine-thirty in the morning. I inherited the show from Shane Ritchie, who in turn, took over from Danny Baker. So now I'm rubbing shoulders with the mainstream glitteratti, and you know what?

They're perfectly nice folk. No horns, no cloven hooves, no black shirts. Just a bunch of people trying to entertain.

A bunch of people trying not to be car washers any more.

"I'm the king of the heap!"

7
Jeremy Hardy
...'Sex and Drugs and...'

If comedy is the new rock 'n' roll, then I am probably the new Roger Whittaker. But is it? What is the evidence? Was comedy invented by blacks and stolen by whites? Possibly. Is comedy success more to do with packaging and fashion than talent? Probably. Do comedians start out looking all right and then dress like arseholes as soon as they make a bit of money? Arguably. Do we talk bollocks in interviews? Is the Pope Catholic? Yes, and that upbringing is the key to understanding his comedy.

There are, it should be stressed, several striking differences between comedy and rock 'n' roll. Most noticeably, many rock stars don't take themselves entirely seriously and some have a keen sense of humour. Very few, on the other hand, feel the need to be intensely private, appear complex or nurture private torment. Many do succeed in appearing wild, hard or cool, which no comic should attempt. Rock musicians are never called upon to explain why they became rock musicians, and no one ever says that playing an instrument is the most difficult job in the world.

So whence arose the notion that comedy was the true successor to what was presumably thought to be a dead artform? It must have been a journalist who first suggested a link, and that person was fully entitled to do so. It's an angle and everyone's got to eat. The trouble is, although that writer was probably up against a deadline at the time and has long since forgotten penning the words, an alarming number of people have taken them seriously. TV Light Entertainment people now use the expression 'rock 'n' roll' as an approving adjective, along with 'happening' and 'inyerface', in the same earnest and clueless way that aunties say 'with-it' and 'snazzy'.

Comedians are only too ready to believe that we are rock 'n' roll. In fairness, there are connections. It's probably true to say that 'alternative' comedy arose because of the effect that punk had on poetry, fringe theatre and student revue. And the early days saw genuine cross-overs. John Dowie, who long preceded the alternative comedy explosion/revolution/movement/phenomenon, and towered above it until he got sick of performing, was recording songs with Factory Records. Ronnie Golden came to comedy via the Fabulous Poodles. From Bristol, the experimental genius Paul B Davies toured his band Shoes for Industry while also writing and producing the work of Crystal Theatre, which nurtured the talents of Keith Allen and Andrew Bailey.

But although punk put irony and humour back into rock 'n' roll, and its effect on the other arts could only be healthy, by the late 1980s the music business was all serious, slick and professional again. So, by 1990, to say a comedian was 'rock 'n' roll' was to say he was balding, business-like, expensively but tastelessly clad, and clinging to a rather tragic sense that he was genuinely outrageous. America saw the emergence of 'Outlaw Comics': ungainly-looking men in early middle age, strutting unconvincingly in cowboy boots and black silk shirts, decrying the effeminacy of pop and quite certain that they were controversial. It was comedy's attempt at hard rock and like the original, while wanting desperately to be hard, it was camp, showy and more than faintly ludicrous.

Unfortunately but inevitably, the movement, though slight, reverberated in this country. Confusingly, at about the same time, rock 'n' roll suddenly fulfilled all those promises about never dying, and started a bit of a revival. There were indie bands all over the place, rap and grunge – oh forget it, it's obvious I have no idea what I'm talking about, but you know what I mean: Rock 'n' Roll suddenly got all rock 'n' roll again. Essential to the legend that comedy was the new Rock 'n' Roll was that the old one was finished, and it clearly wasn't.

So, rather than trying to replace it, comedians have sought to associate themselves with it. Comics want to hang out with musicians, to see their photographs in the same magazines. They talk about bands, link their names with them, do interviews with the music press. And the media are happy to oblige. *Top Of The Pops* is now presented by comics. Radio stations recruit on the cabaret circuit instead of head-hunting hospital DJs. And there are whole magazines devoted to comedy, or rather, the subject of comedy; they are not funny magazines, they are pornography for those unhealthily fixated with comedians. *Family Circle* contains more wit and it's cheaper.

In terms of media coverage, comedy *has* replaced rock 'n' roll. It generates an absurdly unwarranted amount of attention. I'm sure that even the *Pharmacist's Quarterly* lists who's performing Upstairs at Weston's the Chemist, on Streatham High Road, every other Tuesday. And there is always at least one late-night comedy showcase to be found on the telly, breaking the rockingest new comics of the moment, alienating all us thirty-somethings who sit shaking our heads and saying: 'But they all sound exactly the same.' And, it has to be said, that I am writing now *about* comedy, in a book whose antecedent was called *Rock Talk*.

So what am I complaining about? Nothing. really. Only that I am way past being fashionable. Of course I'd be delighted if Sleeper started turning up at my gigs, happier still if the Chieftains asked me to appear in their new video. But thankfully, I am sufficiently grounded to age with grace. I shan't grow my hair or sport a goatee, wear leather trousers or run around the stage shouting. I shan't wear a Damon-from-Blur fringe, because I'm old enough to have had fringes that were enforced by barbers selling reusable condoms who asked your dad how you wanted your hair cut. I shall just keep gigging and recording, immune to fashion, with loyal fans and even some youngsters getting into it, doing what I've always done and doing it well.

Oh no. I'm the new Status Quo.

8
Arnold Brown
...'No Accounting For Comedy'

I was always very interested in comedy, even before I became an accountant. Perhaps my background had a lot to do with it. As I used to say in my act: 'I'm Scottish and Jewish. Two stereotypes for the price of one. Perhaps the best value in the West End tonight... perhaps not'.

Being Jewish had a very powerful effect on my comedy; after all, the link between comedy and Jewishness is based on 2,000 years of punchlines. The Hebrew Holy Book, *The Talmud*, is written in a story-telling moralistic style and over the years this has influenced comedians like Lenny Bruce, Woody Allen and Jackie Mason, who used to be a rabbi.

My own comedy career started on the writing side, in a low-key manner. In the early 1970s, I was working as an accountant in London, and as a hobby, I used to write one-liners for BBC Radio 4's *Week Ending* programme. I'd take my jokes in to their office on Friday mornings on my way to work. Then, thanks to Ted Heath's battle with the miners, ending in the four-day week, I found I had much more time to get on with the writing. During this period I bumped into writers like David Renwick (who later wrote *One Foot In The Grave*) and producers such as John Lloyd, of *Blackadder* fame.

Gradually I began to write for other shows. I contributed a sketch or two to a strange, surreal radio programme called *Lines From My Grandfather's Forehead*. Harold Pinter used to contribute pieces, and it a won a Light Entertainment Programme Of The Year award. I had some lines used in BBC TV's *Not The Nine O'Clock News*. Pamela Stephenson read one of my lines as a news item: 'After hearing about over-crowding in prisons, Margaret Thatcher says that long-term inmates should be encouraged to buy their own cells.'

I had come to London from Glasgow in the early '60s, and frequented a restaurant in Swiss Cottage, where all the pseudo-intellectuals like myself used to hang out. Every Saturday morning I would go in there with my *New Yorker* under my arm and pretend to be Lenny Bruce. There were a handful of us who used to go there to have meals and to talk. Even then, and without realising what I was doing, I began timing my interruptions so as to get the best comedic effect

In 1978 a friend returned from New York, where he'd been running a small comedy club in The Village. One evening I went in to a coffee bar in Swiss Cottage and he was trying out some material on a tiny stage, but someone in the audience kept heckling and interrupting him. For some reason I rushed up on stage and – although I didn't have any jokes prepared – I tried to put this heckler down on behalf of my friend. In the process I had my own ego-trip. That was my first attempt at stand-up comedy...

I was always very interested in comic improvisation. All my comedy until my Swiss Cottage début was unformed and very much of the moment. Usually it took the form of these spontaneous conversations in coffee bars. One day, in my lunch hour, I went along to an improvisation group called the Theatre Machine. They invited volunteers up from the audience, and as I went on stage, I deliberately tripped, so as to get a laugh. I was getting better all the time...

I also used to listen to records by Nichols and May, who were an American improvisation duo of the '70s. They got their ideas in much the same way as Peter Cook and Dudley Moore did for their Derek And Clive stuff. I started taping improvisation sketches in my flat in Hampstead, purely for the amusement of my friends and myself.

At round about the same time, I joined a comedy writing group led by a mainstream writer called Brad Ashton, who used to write for Mike and Bernie Winters, Dick Emery and Les Dawson. We'd have celebrity writers like Denis Norden lecturing us about the nuts and bolts of comedy. One day, Brad mentioned that there was a new club opening in the West End called the Comedy Store.

Part of the deal at the Comedy Store was that you had to go along beforehand and register your name, just like at the Job Centre. It turned out to be my Youth Opportunity Scheme, even though I was over 40 at the time. Comedy is all about atmosphere and the Gargoyle Club, tucked away in Meard Street, off Dean Street in Soho, was perfect for the birth of alternative comedy. Decades before, socialites like the Prince Of Wales used to wine and dine there and take in the shows. By May 1979 it had become a strip club, run by a businessman called Don Ward, who had once been a stand-up comedian. The idea for the Comedy Store came from his partner, Peter Rosengard, who had been inspired by similar clubs he'd seen on a visit to the States. Peter was – and is – a madcap, impulsive guy who recently made the *Guinness Book Of Records* as the man who sold the largest life insurance policy.

The Opening Night was exciting and crazy. The audience were plied with free champagne, and there were all sorts of media people everywhere. I particularly remember two guys from two different radio stations interviewing each other. The infamous gong was used in those days, and an unknown college lecturer called Alexei Sayle was compère.

My stand-up début was somewhat less than successful. I was so naive, I didn't realise you had to have prepared material. I really did think that you just made it up as you went along. I had one joke: 'Good evening, my name is Arnold Brown and I'm an accountant, I check things...' and I was about to say 'Can you hear me at the back?' when someone shouted out, 'We can't hear you at the back', and that was the end of my act. I was gonged off.

A crew from BBC TV's *Newsnight* were there, because they'd wanted to do a piece on 'the accountant who wants to be a comedian'. I remember them asking me: 'Does this mean that you're discouraged?' and quick as a flash I replied, with show business bravado: 'No, I'll be back tomorrow night.' And I was.

That opening night was particularly exciting because it explored totally uncharted territories. Nowadays there is so much emphasis placed on the rules of comedy, but back then no one knew what was going to happen next. There was a guy called David Day who used to play the piano in a funny/terrible way; he used to do 15 minutes and the audience would boo and hiss him, but he'd carry on. And there'd be the eccentrics, like the guy who used to be an art gallery attendant. People would turn up once, perform, and you'd never see them again. It was full of outlandish people who didn't belong anywhere else. There was no pressure to hone your act, because people expected it to be all over the place. It was a fragmented, disturbing atmosphere, and the use of the gong didn't help. It was eventually dropped because it proved too disruptive.

Bit by bit I started, literally, to 'get my act together'. My old catch-phrase, 'Why not?', started off as a way of dealing with my lack of material. It gave me a few precious seconds in which to collect my thoughts. But then Barry Norman said 'Why not?' on his television programme once, and Rory Bremner picked up on it. This was long after I'd made it my own (or at least I thought I had), but everyone started assuming I'd nicked it from Rory, so I had to ditch it. Ah, the injustice of it all. It was also useful to have a suitable heckle put-down line, something every stand-up comedian finds essential. Mine was: 'Do I hear the long-term side effects of Junior Aspirin?'

I've never been part of the 'Have you ever noticed...' school of comedy. I prefer my humour to come from my own perspective: comedy that could only happen to me. Admittedly it's very self-centred, but that's the way it is. My criterion for good comedy is that if someone else can do your material, then it's not that funny. Norman Lovett is a prime example of someone who can create his own world. No one else could ever do Norman's material, it's something that's very personal to him. I have always admired comedians who invent themselves like that, whether it be Billy Connolly, Alexei Sayle, Jeremy Hardy or Harry Hill.

One of my early one-liners in stand-up was about the deprivation in Glasgow under the Conservatives: 'The two year waiting list for people who want to vandalise telephone kiosks.' And, of course, the problem of being Jewish in Glasgow: 'No football team to support'.

Another important strand in my comedy is, like many other comedians, my relationship with my father. I used to tell a joke about the shame we suffered in Glasgow because he was a teetotaller, and the disgrace on Saturday nights of him being thrown *into* pubs. As I lived in north-west London, I made jokes about the contrast between how trendy Hampstead is as opposed to Glasgow. About how people in Hampstead council houses have a second council house in Wales they go to at the weekend. It was so nice in Hampstead, we used to call it NW-Twee. This use of absurd contrast is another element to my comedy.

Before 1979, stand-up in this country was mainly apolitical. Comedians attacked the government, and it didn't matter which party happened to be in power. Comedy was largely stereotypical, dominated by sexism and racism, but the Comedy Store changed the agenda for ever.

In many ways, Alexei Sayle was the mainstay of the fledgling New Comedy scene. He had already been part of Alternative Cabaret, a group of alternative comedians and folk singers, who used to appear together in London pubs. Other members included Jim Barclay, Tony Allen, Andy de la Tour, Pauline Melville and Maggie Steed (who wore a diaphragm on her head and talked about birth control). Tony Allen in particular was very influenced by Lenny Bruce and by Ladbroke Grove politics. He had lovely jokes about undercover drugs squad officers, who were easy to spot because they were selling at 1965 prices.

Another prime player in the early days was Keith Allen. He came on stage totally naked, covering his parts with a carrier bag. He had a great line about going into the countryside for the first time, and how he'd never before seen a horse without a policeman on top. There was a tendency at the time to be more working-class than you actually were, and it was rumoured that Keith had been to a minor public school. Andy de la Tour was also very politically radical: I remember him doing a routine about Airey Neave just after the MP had been blown up by the INLA. Of course there were other important arrivals on the scene: Rik Mayall and Ade Edmondson, Nigel Planer and Peter Richardson, and a hyperactive dynamo called Ben Elton.

My daily routine was schizophrenic: by day working as an accountant, by night performing at The Comedy Store. One evening in October 1979, I went on after all the drunks had gone home, to about 50 or 60 people. They just let me go on and on. I improvised through 45 minutes of stuff. It was a dream, it had never happened before – and (so far) it's never happened since. Later that night, Keith Allen created a scene at the Comedy Store reception desk by insisting that I got paid. That £10 was the first money I'd ever made out of comedy.

In October 1980 I got a telephone call from Peter Richardson. 'We're having a meeting about starting a new

group called the Comic Strip,' he told me. 'Are you interested?'
I was.

Alexei was again the compère, and I joined Ade, Rik,
Peter and Nigel in the Comic Strip. I suppose my role was to be
the quiet *ying* to their manic *yang*. As time went on, we invited
along guests like Ben Elton, Keith Allen, and The Heebee-
Geebees, featuring among others Angus Deayton. Four months
after we started, I remember listening to the audition of a
young female duo called French & Saunders.

It was almost as if comedy was the new punk – for the
others, at least. I stuck out like a sore thumb, a tenuous bridge
between the old school of comedy (as represented by the Chic
Murray Scottish droll) and the new, anarchic style. I suppose I
linked the avant garde of the old with the new. My function at
the Comic Strip has been to provide 50 laid-back, slow-burning
one-liners in my 17-minute spot. That wouldn't work these
days: now it's much more like McDonald's comedy. Humour
on demand.

Like the Comedy Store, the Comic Strip was based in a
Soho strip club; this time at Raymond's Revue Bar. It became
the trendy place to go. In the audience were people like the
Pythons, Barry Humphries and Dave Allen. One night Jack
Nicholson turned up with Bianca Jagger. The next day the
tabloids carried a ridiculous story about how Jack had been
shocked by this 'band of smut merchants' (ie, us). Another
evening I went out into the corridor after my act and was surprised to see Dustin Hoffman walking towards me. As he
passed me on his way to the washroom, he told me something I
will never forget: 'Comedy's important,' he said.

It was a very different type of comedy to that practised
at the Comedy Store, which had a very impromptu style, and
where you were free to do whatever you wanted. At the Comic
Strip, the acts virtually did the same routines every show,
because that's what audiences demanded.

Initially we performed six nights a week, and twice on Friday and Saturdays. The run at Raymond's Revue Bar lasted ten months and in 1981 and '82, we toured the UK playing rock venues, colleges and arts centres. By the end of '82 the live Comic Strip had disbanded and *The Young Ones* exploded on to our TV screens. I stuck with my day job for two more years, and then I finally took the plunge and became a full-time stand-up comedian.

I went on to win the Perrier Award in 1987, and in 1990, I supported Frank Sinatra at an open-air gig at Ibrox Park, as part of the Glasgow European City Of Culture celebrations. As I told the audience, I suggested to Frank that his opening song should be *Fly Me To Dunoon*...

John Cleese and I – there I go, name-dropping again – recently took part in a conference about psycho-analysis and humour at the Comedy Store, organised by the Freud Museum. (For my part, it's much easier to talk about comedy than it is to do it.) There were over 300 psychiatrists and psychologists there, and I opened with the line: 'Being the audience you are, I want to tell you in advance that if there's anything you don't understand, please regard it as significant.'

I have taken my one-man show to the Edinburgh Fringe most years, and in '94, I based it on my book, *Are You Looking At Me, Jimmy?* (Methuen). The hero of the piece is my Uncle Harry. Let me tell you what kind of person he was. Smoking has always been a very emotive subject but in the '50s and '60s no one realised the dangers. But Harry knew. Thirty years ago, he said that the best way to alert the public to the risks was to bury all smokers in packs of tens and twenties. That's the kind of family I come from.

Like most comedians I try and write a stack of new material every year. I relish life's contrasts. Billy Connolly, for example, is also Scottish, but comes from a completely different background to myself. His reference points are the shipyards, heavy drinking and vomiting (sorry to bring that up), whereas I'm a far quieter, more gentle kind of guy. He talks about murdering a curry, I talk about dominating a cream cake.

That's the kind of comedian I am.

King Arthur and the knights of the Algonquin Round table...

"...and Sir Gawain – have you any finely tuned epigrams or withering critical put-downs for us this afternoon?"

9
Jon Ronson
...'Funny'.

Dalston, East London. Sunday.

Okay. How come nobody has ever heard of the authors of those books advertised in *The Guardian* called *Learn To Be A Successful Writer*? This is the joke I have today composed in advance for a workshop I'm attending entitled: 'How To Be A Successful Stand-Up Comedian' (tutor: Mr Reg Wilkinson). Reg telephoned me earlier this week to inform me that, whilst he is pleased to have me witness his work in a journalistic capacity, I must be prepared to join in and be funny too.

'I'm not having you sit there like a lemon,' he explained. 'Everybody has to write one joke in advance, and you're no exception.'

'I've got a busy week,' I replied, 'so I may not have time. In fact, I'm having a vasectomy tomorrow.'

'Are you?' said Reg.

'Yes,' I replied. 'The doctor said: "Are you having it done privately?" I said: "I bloody hope so!" Will that do?'

'No,' replied Reg. 'Come up with a better one.'

Although Reg has been teaching these courses for three years, today' s workshop (situated in a youth drop-in centre in Dalston, part of their Comedy Weekend For Underprivileged Kids: clowns, jesters. Comic Relief and so on) is unique. The group is made up entirely of local young offenders and estate-kids, and the aim is not only to teach them how to amuse professionally, but also how to use comedy as a weapon against local bullies. Swipe 'em down with a gag, smack 'em in the face with a well-aimed wisecrack when cornered in a darkened walkway by a dozen crack-addled lunatics, etc.

'Comedy can be a very potent weapon,' explains Reg. 'It can get you out of all sorts of scrapes.'

It is, in fact, in a darkened walkway on the way to the workshop that I cornered by an ominous-looking young boy called Steve. A large part of Dalston appears to be one of those districts that values it's architectural layout over it's population, and I have taken a wrong turning and stumbled into a maze of portentous alleyways and underpasses. As I'm about to give up hope, a young man steps out from the shadows.

'I'm looking for the youth club,' I say. 'Can you help me?'

'Are you a comedian?' he snaps.

'No, no,' I begin to hastily stammer. 'I'm being serious. I'm looking for the youth club. I know I'm too old for a youth club but...'

'Yeah yeah.' he quickly interrupts. 'The comedy workshop.' That's what I mean. I'm a comedian too. Follow me.

So Steve leads me through the walkways, through the stench of urine and viciously scrawled graffiti, swapping small-talk.

'They're thinking of bringing out a stamp with John Major's face on the front, he begins.

'Are they?' I say.

'Fucking right,' he replies. 'They fucking are. But they can't.'

'Why not?' I say.

'Because,' he replies, 'people keep spitting on the wrong side.' Steve gives me a steely glare. 'That's very. very funny. ' I say.

'It is, isn't it?' he replies. 'And did you know that an

anagram of Ted Heath's name is The Death?'

'That's very funny.' I say.

'I know,' he replies. 'Anagrams of people's names are very funny. Jim Morrison – Mr Mojo Risin'.'

'Noj Nosnor,' I say. 'That's mine.'

'That's not funny,' says Steve. 'That's bollocks.'

'You're right,' I say. 'It's bollocks.'

Pretty soon we arrive at the youth club and meet Reg, a bearded man in his mid-forties. The turnout is small – six of us altogether – sitting on wooden chairs in an austere room with a broken window. For an hour, Reg lectures us on timing, structure and context. Then he calls upon us to present our pre-prepared jokes. Steve is first. Nervously, he stands and coughs.

'Um,' he begins. 'My family is so poor that …um…'

'Take your time,' says Reg softly. Steve wrings his hands, looking as if he's about to cry.

'Um… so poor that…' There is a long silence. Steve sits down.

'That's fine.' says Reg. 'Jon?'

'How come nobody's ever heard of those books in *The Guardian* called *How To Be A Successful Writer?*' I quickly mutter, staring at the floor.

'Great.' says Reg. 'Suzie?'

Suzie, a tenacious sixteen year old, stands up with ill-disguised fury in her eyes.

'You know those tampon adverts,' she yells angrily. 'Everyone's always horse-riding and swimming. It makes you think that everyone just goes horse-riding when their periods arrive.' She pauses, and adds: 'Stupid.'

'Great.' says Reg.

'Um,' I interject, sheepishly. 'Not the books. I mean the writers of the books. Nobody's heard of…'

'And something else,' screams Suzie, glaring at me. 'How come they use BLUE liquid in the demonstrations? Blood isn't BLUE. It's fucking RED! Stupid.'

'That's great.' says Reg. 'Well done. It's funny, you see, because it's true.'

A tea break is called, and I notice Steve approaching Reg, whispering in his ear.

'Steve wants another go,' announces Reg when we reconvene. And everyone nods supportively. With palpable pain in his eyes, Steve stands.

'My family,' he says, 'is so poor that...'

He looks around the room, and we glance away, casually.

'...so poor that when it's cold we all sit around a candle. And when it's REALLY cold we light it.'

'Very funny,' we all say. 'That's very funny.'

Later that day.

And here we are now, backstage at Dalston Holy Trinity Church's 49th annual Clown Service – down the road from the workshop, another event in Dalston's Underprivileged Kids Comedy Weekend. I am surrounded by 100 clowns, honking their horns, falling over banana skins, and so on. 100 clowns and 50 photographers, crowded into a tiny back room. It is a media circus *(honk! honk!)*, a frenzy of organised pathos. The vicar, John Willard, is attempting to smile amiably through the chaos, but the tension on his face is palpable.

'Excuse me,' he announces.' 'Um. Excuse me. I have an announcement to make...'

'Announcement! Announcement!' yells Fizzy-Lizzy The Clown, honking her horn.

'Anouncey-nouncy! Mousey Mousey Mousey!' screams Billy The Clown, his bow-tie flashing.

As impressive as the turn out is today, however, the numbers are way down on last year; which was, in turn, was down on the year before. Like the Armistice Day commemorations, this venerable event is tinged with woeful statistics. The clowns are dying off, and those that are left are almost certainly crying on the inside.

The main photo-opportunity, in fact, is reserved for the very old end very ailing Smokey The Clown, who's attendance here succeeds in single-handedly personifying the lamentable demise of a cherished British tradition: a very old clown praying in a church while clutching a Union Jack in his timeworn, grease-paint splattered hands - if only someone had thought to bring along an end of a pier with them, the set would have been complete. Consequently, the photographers flock.

'Ooh,' he wheezes, attempting to cover up his shakily drawn black-ink Smokey The Clown tattoo. 'I'm afraid I can't do somersaults anymore. But hang on…' He fumbles around in his pocket for an age, and eventually retrieves a small plastic comedy spider.

'Ooh,' he says, waving it in front of the cameras. 'Scary. Ooh.' And then he stares forlornly into space for a long time, to the palpable delight of the photographers.

It wasn't always this way, of course. As the century began, clowns stood at the very apex of comedy. There was nothing funnier than falling over, and those who fell over in a professional capacity were rewarded handsomely. As the decades progressed – sadly – the backlash began. First Smokey Robinson suggested that the smiles on their faces were only there just to fool the public (a trivial yet potent slur). Thereafter. Ronald McDonald created an inalienable link between red noses and the bloody genocide of countless cows, and John Osborne successfully implied that they all went home, drank a bottle of whisky, and shouted at their wives. The final nail in the coffin, however, arrived with the awful discovery that serial killer John Wayne Gacy dressed up as a clown (big shoes, bowtie that lit up, and all) when he viciously butchered his young victims. It proved to be an irreparable setback.

Like Santa Claus, who has now been done for child-molestation every Christmas since 1992 (a wretched fact that certainly brings a whole new meaning to the words: 'You better watch out, you better not cry, you better not shout, I'm telling you why...') clowns are nowadays widely considered to be a rather pitiable – and weirdly dangerous – anachronism.

'We're doing this,' explains Rev Willard, 'to show that God can have a jolly good laugh too. We all slip on banana skins in our lives, and when we want to throw a brick-bat at someone, we should stop and put down that brick-bat and lob a well-aimed custard pie instead.'

All metaphored out, Rev Willard wipes his face with a hanky, and gets to the serious business of the day. 'If anyone takes photographs during the service they will be thrown out, and there's no talking or laughing during the prayers. Or you will be thrown out. Clear?' At this, even the clowns look solemn.'

'So you won't make a noise,' he concludes, staring around the room, 'because that would be VERY SELFISH.'

'Oh yes we will!' pipes up a clown at the back.

'Shhhhh,' reply 50 clowns, furiously glaring at him. And there is a long silence.

In the end, however, the service turns out to be gag-packed. The guest vicar delivers an hilarious sermon about child abuse: 'I gut a job in Kennington because I like Missionary work! *(honk! honk!)*... The kids there were so abused that they had Esther Rantzen's home phone number! *(honk! honk!)*... The mothers wouldn't say "I'll set your dad on you," because they didn't know who their dad WAS!' And so on.

Still, it's good to see that God can have a jolly good laugh too. Unfortunately, the sermon is marred slightly by Rev Willard's constant ferocious interruptions: 'You! Girl! Photographer! I EXPRESSLY ordered NO PHOTOGRAPHS! Children. This is a LISTENING TIME. A LISTENING time.

You! Girl! I told you. Out. Now. Out.'

All this intensity is giving me a terrible headache, so I quietly take refuge in a pew near the altar. Suddenly, there is a tap on my shoulder.

'Excuse me,' says a fierce looking lady. 'Are you a clown?'

Shocked, and slightly upset, I look down at my carefully selected casual jumper and trousers.

'No,' I reply, lamely. 'I'm from *The Guardian*.'

'Well go and sit somewhere else,' she snaps.' 'This is for the clowns. It's not very fair, you sitting in a clown's seat. is it? It's not very funny, is it?'

10
John Hegley
...'A short address at the comedy college'

I hope
you will beware of putting comedy
under the microscope.
To dissect it
first you must kill it,
you must lose the thrill, chill it.
I don't wish my fish
to be a fillet.
Would you beach a whale
merely for teaching porpoises?
I don't want to appear
on a graph
and I don't want to dread
what comes after
the laughter's dead
and that's it, I said.
And as I was leaving the class
I fell on my arse.

11
Ronnie Golden
...recalls the time he was branded 'An Evil Purveyor of Filth'

In this business we so lovingly call 'show', the grim spectre of Death is omnipresent. We don't fall, we 'die'; we don't involuntarily laugh, we 'corpse' and a regular topic for discussion whenever comedians congregate is the scene of their most horrible 'death.'

Mine was at The Cliffs Pavilion, Westcliff-on-Sea on Saturday November the 8th, 1985. I was the opening act for a cappella singers The Flying Pickets, a group I had successfully worked with many times before. This was to be my first stand-up show in nearly two months, following an accident when I'd come off my racing bike head-first over the handlebars and subsequently smashed my face into the tarmac. My nose was broken and for the week following the operation my head resembled that of The Elephant Man after his out-of-the-bag experience. When I arrived at the theatre I still had fresh scars, which I attempted to disguise by growing a scrubby beard.

Once in my dressing-room, I pulled my wrinkled and musty stage suit from out of the Sainsbury's carrier-bag and enquired of a passing Picket as to what kind of audience I might expect. 'Crazy,' I was informed, 'really wild.'

I was not fully convinced of this, and, as I checked my reflection in the the mirror I was faced with the apparition of a crumpled, down-at-heel wino, an image compounded, I'm sure, by the quarter bottle of cognac I'd consumed to stave my growing nerves during the train journey down. Comedy, you see, is a muscle that must be flexed regularly in order to stay in condition.

I heard my name announced over the PA system and made my way to the microphone. Instead of my usual opening routine involving a few well-honed lines, I could hear myself launching inappropriately into topics relating to, amongst others, Norman Tebbit and cancer.

The Devil himself, it seemed to me, had taken possession of both my mind and my mouth. I attempted, in vain, to halt the runaway train my act had become but, alas, it was too late. I caught my first glimpse of the audience and saw that I was facing a mass of people as old as seventy and as young as six. Suddenly there was no moisture in my mouth and my speech started to falter. The only reaction to my first seven minutes or so had been shocked silence but now a thorniness was becoming detectable as a few voices expressed their indignation. Then there were more voices and clearly distinguishable words were forming: 'Rubbish!' 'Get off!' and 'Crap!' being just four of them. At this point it occurred to me that not only had I severely 'lost-the-plot' but, worse, that I had found it again in the local cemetery with my name on the headstone.

'Do you want me to go?' I dismally enquired. A question of such sublime pointlessness could only have been uttered by a Prime Minister called Major. Two thousand foaming mouths bayed back to me in the affirmative. Disconsolately I grabbed my bag and guitar and slunk off to my dressing-room. Uproar ensued. I could hear one of The Flying Pickets apologising to the crowd; he then came backstage and cursed me frostily. I left the theatre by the stage door and headed for

the station. With Southend safely behind me, I sobbed helpless-
ly on the journey back convinced that this night's debacle was
the harbinger of further failure, penury, and the spiralling vor-
tex of madness. But then, having virtually stabbed my self-
esteem to death, I attempted to rally myself. OK., it was a disaster, the ultimate defeat, but apart from one group of a cappella
singers and a couple of thousand fuming strangers surely no-
one need hear of this Night From Hell.

'Filthy Comic Booed Off,' screamed the front page of the
Southend Evening Echo the following week. The story also made
small corners of the national Sundays.

'Ronnie Golden will never again work on the same
stage as The Flying Pickets.' (The Flying Pickets).

'He is banned for life from performing in this theatre'
(EF Mundy, Manager Cliffs Pavilion).

Apart from a supportive phone call from Picket Brian
Hibberd I was being publicly rubbished by a group of people I
had, until then, felt a strong affinity with.

Now, dear reader, let me take you forward in time to
January 1991. I am master-of-ceremonies at a star-studded bill
at The Duke of York's Theatre in London's West End, proceeds
to Amnesty International. The atmosphere in the theatre is
warm expectation and I am, I have to say, 'firing on all cylin-
ders.' Having noted that a certain singing group was on the
bill, I'd dug out my old 'obituary' from the *Southend Evening
Echo*.

I show it to the audience and precis my woe-filled saga
to general guffaws. I then recall the line about never working
on the same stage etc, and announce the next act: '...and how
wrong they were, because here are the people responsible for
that statement, ladies and gentlemen... The Flying Pickets!'
Enter stage left: one embarrassed Picket line.

The next and, you'll be relieved to hear, dear reader,
final stop on this ride of redemption occurs on November 11th,

1993, when yours truly has been booked into – guess where? – yes, The Cliffs Pavilion. I am reaching the end of a month-long tour as opening act for Don McLean. No, not the toothsome *Crackerjack* presenter, but Don 'I-could've-told-you-Vincent-if-you-hadn't-cut-yer-bleedin'-ear-off' McLean. For the second time since the Night from Hell I tucked my dog-eared copy of the *Echo* in my bag and, as my performance had been greeted with a warm and appreciative reaction, I feel duty-bound to produce it, quoting the comment made by the manager about me never appearing in his theatre again.

Having taken leave of the stage I was told that he had been in the audience with several governors of the theatre and had not recognised me until my exposé. When he realised that I was the same 'evil purveyor of filth', he apparently flew into a rage and refused payment to both myself and Don McLean's management on the grounds that they should have known that I was banned for life. I mean, blimey, child molesters only get ten years! They, of course, had to succumb and payment was duly made. I left the theatre through the same door I had exited from almost exactly eight years earlier. Then it had been in humiliation; now it was in exultation. Once again, the intrepid comedian had cheated death and I could feel my heart beat with the rhythm of mischievous victory.

Revenge *is* sweet, let no-one tell you different. It is also (if I may paraphrase) a dish best served cold.

12
Peter Curran
...'Five Years In A PC Camp'

I had already thanked Bernard Manning for being on the show, when he said: 'hang on Pete, you're Irish - you'll love this one: "Paddy goes into a mini-cab office..."' and as the Lard of the North chuckled his way towards the inevitable conclusion, I found myself laughing. The joke itself would have left even the most gormless idiot po-faced, but the fact than Manning was prepared to sally forth and enjoy his intrusion on to the stamping ground of the Politically Correct was funny.

The curious thing about 'PC' is that it has always felt like a bolt-on accessory to social living. Our suspicion of politicians, our distaste at the ruthless pursuit of profit by privatised public utilities are both born out of experience. But when PC arrived – ready or not – we set loose the thought police inside our own heads. It became important to be seen and heard to use the right buzz words – you could be a roaring Nazi on your own in the car, but when there were others around one felt 'empowered' to illustrate one's sensitivity to the feelings of others. Thankfully, this didn't involve any direct action to change the world. As long as you had acquitted yourself at work or with friends over the dinner table, you could feel that your words spoke more than actions.

The whole nature of mainstream comedy has shifted on its axis during the last 15 years. Women were once either nags or potential crumpet, whereas now they are long-suffering souls that put up with immature men who do not know how to please them (it still helps if you are pretty, naturally). Men are either tormented souls governed by the beast beneath the belly-button or insensitive brutes. Reality may have bitten comedy, but has this meant bigger laughs? Yes, for a while, but eventually one yawns as yet another joke or sketch buckles under the weight of the new comedy commandments.

The real reason why the Tarbucks of this world lost their grip on prime time was not because their jokes were sexist, racist and politically incorrect; it was because their material had become threadbare. For all the apparent 'openness' of recent comedy, the modern version of stereotypes from Tarbyshire is already wearing thin. Lady Thatcher has a lot to answer for, not least the bleating alternative comedians who accused her of 'acting like a man'.

During our heated encounter, Bernard Manning told me that he didn't tell jokes about disabled people because 'that was cruel'. He was happy to tell jokes about 'ethnics' as they were part of the diverse culture of Great Britain. I'll leave Bernard's gracious assumption that disabled people are more to be pitied than laughed at. There is some validity in his belief that people of all races should be represented on the target range. The zealots of Political Correctness exclude ethnic minorities from the mouths of comedians, unless of course the artist is from that particular minority. Frank Carson and Eddie Murphy have done so much for their people, dontchaknow?

In an ideal world we should all be able to laugh with, and at, each other. Unfortunately, since that Biblical day when Cain noticed that Abel was comparatively loaded, people have used differences to keep their fellow humans down. The problem with Bernard Manning's jokes about minorities is that they are delivered to an audience who remain ignorant about every person's desire for equality. His gags will be the cement that holds prejudices about 'funny foreigners' together.

Politically Correct comedy, from Ben Elton to his more diluted disciples, constantly has to refer to an enemy. The vulgarity and subsequent heartache of the late '80s has meant most of us have got wise to how the world works. This is the time for imagination, not dogma. As for the age-old taboos in the sexist and racist wardrobe, perhaps men and women from every race, creed, and colour should be taken at gunpoint to Wembley Stadium and be forced to listen to a selection of jokes at their expense. it could be organised like jury service, only everyone would be found guilty.

So what has happened since the silencing of the one about the black fella, the mother-in-law and the poof? Some entertainers have invented a comic world around their own experiences. Others tread the light fantastic of surrealism. But what of the entertainer who lacks imagination? During childhood the word 'fuck' is the verbal equivalent of a punch. But these days there is incessant verbal violence on the stage. People with pygmy-sized comic ability still try to disgust an audience who have come out to laugh. You can easily spot the comic from a stable home: channelling their faint embarrassment at their background and the frustration they feel at not being truly creative into a red-faced tirade from the stage.

What about a little bit of politics? There are few performers who can still deal successfully in the currency of political humour. Like trying to figure out why you've got a hangover, it's all too obvious.

Still,there is always childhood; fond remembrance and affectionate guffaws guaranteed. Entertainers have sucked the marrow from the bones of childhood experiences. From Spangles to Slinkies, our memories have been worked to the point of exhaustion. Maybe this is a good thing for the future of comedy to live in the present. The fixed security of the past is such a tempting context for humour, that all of us want to look back from the uncertain vantage point of the present. I can hardly wait to be able to wet myself about the information superhighway in the not too distant future.

Political Correctness was bound to loosen its grip on comedy and everyday life. The whole concept is an intellectual one; it's all head and no belly laughs. Beneath the surface of a right-on comedian there lurks either a stunted personality or a ribald, salacious monster from the old school of fun. There is an equilibrium beginning to settle where the sexes acknowledge differences and can taunt each other playfully rather than aggressively. There are some sad individuals who have even resorted to good old-fashioned sexist humour on stage, but of course they are being ' post -modern' about it.

When it come to race, the smile fades. Unfortunately, the people who wrestle with the injustice of racism or who simply abhor it are in a minority. Most people in this country simply don't have the inclination to worry about it. Comedy about racism is shared among the converted, for the vast majority of people who like a laugh, they have as much interest in it as Paul Calf has in foreplay. For entertainers who do tackle racism, it is seldom funny – more polemic than gag, because the performer is burdened by the apathy of the majority out in the real world. This is not to say that racist or sexist comedy has been expunged from the comedy circuit. Comedians and audiences may steer clear of blacks, Asians, women and Irish, but who needs them when you have 'stupid Americans', 'drunken Australians' and 'ugly bitches like Virginia Bottomley' to laugh at. The television show *The Real McCoy* has a few great characters and sketches created by black and Asian performers, so why haven't some of the cast been seen in other guises on television? Their appearance as part of *Fry and Laurie's Christmas Night With The Stars* had echoes of 20 years ago when the cast of *Porgy And Bess* might have been invited to sing in the middle of an all-white variety show.

Still, we've all tried on our mum's knickers, haven't we?

The element of surprise, the most long-lasting comic effect, has been ill-served by Political Correctness. I now have a knowledge of 'periods' far in excess of my five sisters. I sit, mirthless, as the subject of premature ejaculation comes early and often from the stage.

The biggest, most heinous, crime committed in the name of PC is the empowerment of the articulate heckler. Whatever happened to 'Bollocks!' or 'You're shit, get off!'? Nowadays, comedian and audience have to suspend proceedings while the heckler repeats an inaudible paragraph of criticism, often so profound or obscure that the performer will be lucky to get his or her own act back on the rails again. It is only a matter of time before too many friends say the magic words, 'You're really funny, why don't you have a go?' and Nightmare Heckler gets to open the show next week. Still, at least he or she is out of the audience.

'I've got the hang of it at last.'

13
Paul Whitehouse
...on 'Questions...'

The biggest job in comedy is answering questions. When you're at home, people from newspapers and magazines ring up all the time and ask you things. And when you go out, perfect strangers stop you in the street and throw posers at you. They ask things like: 'how did you get involved in comedy?', 'what's the worst question you've ever been asked?' and 'do you always shop at Safeways?' Some even want to know what your favourite meal is. And they're not all waiters.

So, in no particular order, here are the answers to some frequently-asked (and some rarely-asked) questions. If you are ever tempted to accost me in the street and quiz me on my taste in socks or on which shampoo I use, may I caution you against it? Please?

How did you get involved in comedy?
Harry Enfield used to come down my pub and even sleep on my sofa. Not only did he abuse my hospitality, but he also nicked all my humorous lines and characters while I was asleep. I therefore put a horseless head in his bed, which wasn't a great idea as he was still sleeping on my sofa at the time and it took ages to clean up. But he got the point, and insisted I wrote with him. Then I obviously needed a girl to type for me, so I employed Charlie Higson.

What was the first funny line you wrote?

The first line Harry used of mine was for his Hoffnung character, Sir Harry Stocracy. It was: 'Oh, I love a nice cup of tea. I'm a proper little fucker for a cuppa.'

How do you you and Charlie Higson write together?

I come up with all the original ideas, and Charlie is a socially dysfunctional plodder who just says, 'but surely the joke is...' all the time.

Are there any comedy tips you want to pass on?

No. Don't be a fool. This is my livelihood.

Okay, then. Have you any advice for people aspiring to a career in comedy?

Keep it funny. Keep it short. Send it to me.

Why do you do it?

It's fun.

What is the most important part of what you do?

Writing, without a doubt.

What caused you to shift from writing to performing and writing?

The fact that performing is more important than writing.

What makes you laugh?

Reeves and Mortimer, Alan Partridge, Pete and Dud and Monty Python.

What's the funniest thing you've ever done?

Rude Gardener.

What's the funniest thing you've seen or heard?

My mate Martin Bentley, an accident prone ex-plasterer.

What's the worst piece of gossip you've heard about yourself?

The reality has always been far worse than the gossip.

What's the worst piece of gossip you've heard about someone else?

That Stevie Nicks has cocaine blown up her arse (nice work if you can get it).

Does working in America appeal?

Not really.

Do you consider any subject unsuitable for comedy?

Yes... But I don't want to sound wet, so, no.

How does a television programme get made?

You take an idea to someone, they have an opinion on how to do it better, even though they didn't think it up; you go to another meeting where someone else tells you how to do it better and so on. If you're lucky enough to get it commissioned you rehearse with the rest of the cast, producer, etc., each one of whom are every bit as much of a wanker as yourself. You film it with cameras, you argue endlessly with everyone in the editing suite, it goes out, you get crucified and you realise every one in those original meetings was right.

Do you find your work satisfying?

I enjoy the work (doing it) But not always the work (finished product) A lot of it is deeply bad.

What doesn't make you laugh?

People trying too hard. Smug political humour. And Johnny Observa stuff: '...you know what it's like, yeah, when you...'

Do you worry about people not laughing at your material?

Yes, but if nobody laughs we generally repeat it until they do, or want to kill us.

Are there any lofty theories you want to pass on?

Overthrow the bourgeoisie by means of the armed proletariat seizing control of the means of production... I've only just thought of this one it might need a bit of work.

Tell me a joke.

Absolutely not.

Please.

No.

What's the best question you've been asked?

Journalist: 'Now, Paul, you're one half of the Mary Whitehouse experience aren't you?'

What is the worst question you've ever been asked?
All the above.

What is your favourite meal?
Indonesian, anything chickeny, must include something peanut-topped and rice with a coconut tinge.

What is funny?
I'm bored with comedy.

14
Glen Colson

...remembers Viv Stanshall (1943-1995) 'What *was* he like!'

Whether backstage at London Zoo or ordering a pair of octagonal glasses, there was always something very odd about this ginger geezer; but in between snoozing and boozing, Viv actually fitted quite a bit into his fifty-two years.

It's 1968 and my sister tells me of this Bonzo man who orders her to buy 50 bluebottles for a TV show, *Do Not Adjust Your Set*. Soon I am eating vindaloo and drinking brandy with him. On a good day he'd call me 'Amigo', on a bad day 'Arthur Daley'; and that about summed up our relationship over the last twenty-seven years. Half my gags were scripted by this man… 'Oh really? No, O'Riley!' I still say that once a week.

I don't think that anyone who worked with Viv would deny that he was a genius but his greatest talent was being himself. What a great teacher he was. Over corned-beef sandwiches he'd tell me I was too loutish to become a watercolourist, so it would have to be acrylics – three coats on my willie and nothing could touch me. He could infuriate, yes, but a visit to his snooker club in the Holloway Road and all was forgiven.

He had no truck with politics or sport, but he did play snooker very well indeed, loved nature and was a member of the Zoological Society, where he would take lunch and attend lectures. He liked all his clothes to be handmade by craftsmen; he was mad about books, especially biographies and reference works, and would never let them out of his sight. He would agonise over everything... he was always working on that final draft, hating to let it go. He was a perfectionist.

His flat: an Aladdin's cave of antique daggers, black magic books and handmade instruments, sometimes smelling like a rhino house, at other times like an Indian restaurant. He loved leather handbags, rings of various gemstones and crocodile shoes. He was proud to point out when we dined at Toffs, his local chippy, that his signed photo was up there on the wall, next to the Arsenal football team.

His talents included painting watercolours, oils and acrylics, pottery, carving, etching and – my favourite – making masks from dog-ends. He would paint everything: chairs, cups, walls and toilets. And he talked... I never tired of listening to that wonderful voice, the same one that introduced Horace Bachelor, Princess Anne and J Arthur Rank.

His musical tastes narrowed towards the end but included Glen Shirley, Link Wray and The Fairports. The death of close friends – Moonie, Rebop, BJ Wilson and Ollie Halsall – left deep scars. His last public gig was at the Malt Room, Kendal, on Friday December 20,1991.

When the dust has settled we are all going to miss him like hell. No more Peel sessions, no more outrages, no more late night phone calls. Viv, I hope Mrs E and Scrotum are taking good care of you.

15
Malcolm Hay
...mourns 'Bill Hicks'

The image fitted the man and the kind of material he laid on us. Most of the time Bill Hicks wore black jeans, a black jacket and black boots. Often a black shirt too. He'd pace the stage, lost in thought, puffing on a cigarette. Then he'd stop, lean slightly forwards, thrust his head towards us, as if wanting to share an idea that had just struck him, as though daring anybody to dispute what he was about to say. Yet his stand-up wasn't aggressive. Sure, the thoughts were radical, challenging, uncomfortable. But Hicks delivered them with great good humour and a smile. Sometimes he'd break into a manic laugh. These devilish cackles always marked a moment when he'd overstepped by several miles some boundary of good taste.

Hicks knew that stand-up comics win over an audience by ingratiating themselves in one way or another. So he'd subvert that relationship from the start: 'I've been doing comedy for ten years now, so excuse me while I plaster on a fake smile and plough through this shit once more.' Yet the smile was not a false one. Hicks talked about what mattered to him. The topics were mainly to do with the lunacy of the world we inhabit. That smile simply registered Hicks' horrified amusement at what he'd observed.

He'd talk about pornography and drugs, war and religion. According to Hicks' morality, the first two were okay.

Men are turned on by porn but it doesn't make them rape women. He'd fantasise about the distress he'd cause his parents when, following his sudden and early death, they'd go through his belongings and come across the porno mags. 'Are drugs good?' he'd ask rhetorically. 'No! Some of them are great!' Marijuana shouldn't be legalised – it should be made compulsory. From the stage, then in interviews, Hicks revealed he'd had 'a major drug and alcohol problem' for several years early in his career. After he'd quit both, he said, it was very hard on stage every night for six months. After that, he really began to get his act together.

Some stand-ups crack jokes. Others mix one-liners with more reflective rifts that show something about themselves. Just a few – and Hicks was one – avoid straight gag-telling altogether. 'My philosophy,' Hicks said, 'is fewer jokes and more me.' It was the frankness and honesty that made Hicks' observations funny. One interviewer asked him to describe the nature of his comedy: 'I'm trumpeting my innermost thoughts with an intense smile on my face.'

With supreme command of the art of stand-up too. Hicks could hold a pause so long that the silence would begin to reverberate in your ears. But he'd time it so you'd still be hanging with eager anticipation on his next line. He'd twist his face into an evil smile, a leer, a scowl, a variety of grimaces. He'd act out situations with furious precision, like a mime performer who for once had something real to say. In this way Hicks would make his more exaggerated notions strangely concrete: a moth flying towards the sun, a starving Ethiopian catching a banana dropped from a missile.

Hicks first performed in Britain at the Edinburgh Festival in 1991 He'd long since been branded the bad boy of American stand-up. In that first British show he mocked the false heroics of the American fighting forces in the Gulf War. After all, they'd been insulated against any conceivable danger,

thanks to their vastly superior weaponry. The media propagan-
da had declared the Americans were up against the fourth
largest army in the world. Should we be impressed? Close
behind the Iraqis the Hari Krishnas possessed the fifth largest
army in the world.

What sort of country, Hicks asked, needs a war to make
it feel better about itself? Elsewhere in his shows he'd supply
the answer. A retarded nation. Devoted to consumer goods.
'The third shopping mall from the sun'. 'Have you noticed a
certain anti-intellectualism in this country?' he'd ask. He told
the story of his visit to a Waffle House in Nashville, Tennessee.
'I'm sitting there and I'm eating and I'm reading a book. Right?
I don't know anybody and I'm eating and I'm reading a book.
Fine. A waitress comes over to me. 'What you reading for?' I
said: 'Well, I've never been asked that. Goddammit, you've
stumped me! Not what am I reading, but what am I reading
for? I guess I read for a lot of reasons. But one of the main ones
is so I don't end up being a fuckin' waffle waitress.'

Then a trucker in the next booth gets up, stands over
Hicks, and drawls: 'Well, looks like we got ourselves a reader.
What the hell's going on here?' Hicks exclaims. 'It's like I
walked into a Klan rally in a Boy George costume.' Hicks
reserved some of his most bilious scorn for rednecks. The kind
who race off to the sites of rumoured UFO landings carrying
shotguns. The kind who, while liberals are calling for
'Revolution', are chanting 'Evolution – we want our thumbs.'
Hicks saw himself as an American who loved an America that
didn't exist – a land of freedom and free ideas: 'I subscribe to
the philosophy of gentle anarchy. I believe people are inherent-
ly good, and left to their own devices – with the free exchange
of ideas and information – a joyful lightness would spread
across the face of our dour world.'

In Britain, just like back home, Hicks inspired admira-
tion and hatred in roughly equal measure. Many reviewers, and

most of his audiences would have endorsed the verdict of the *New York Times*: Hicks was 'the most brilliant comic of his generation'. But the right-wing press (that's most of it) mounted a sneer campaign.

In the *Sun* Garry Bushell jeered that 'his attitudes are so '60s he ought to be wearing a kaftan and cowbells'. *The Daily Telegraph* accused Hicks of thinking he had 'a monopoly of concern for just about everything and a licence to season his act with obscenities'. Roughly translated, that means: 'We don't like being lectured at and it's wrong to swear'.

Hicks swore profusely. He swore because he felt strongly about the subjects he was discussing. But he didn't lecture. He'd drive relentlessly towards what he saw as the truth of any situation: 'You see, these things become clear when you talk them out, don't they?' He'd exaggerate for effect. That's at the root of most comedy. The elderly and the terminally ill should be used, Hicks argued, as extras in Schwarzenegger-like action movies. Except they'd get zapped for real. The movies would look great. Those about to die would be assured of going out in a blaze of glory. Hicks's detractors found this sick and offensive. Hicks reckoned it was more offensive to shut people away to die alone in an institution.

His own view of his work was that he was 'taking a reasoned look at a completely unreasonable world'. This was comedy for what Hicks called 'the age of the psycho'. It was no coincidence, he said, that stand-up comedy became big in the States when Reagan was elected as President. The same happened in Britain after the arrival of Thatcher.

It was inevitable that Hicks would be hailed as the new Lenny Bruce. He confessed he was flattered by the comparison. But the thing was he didn't know Bruce's work. 'As far as I can see, he's just a guy who went out there and talked about his life. And, sure, that's what I do.' Like Bruce, Hicks didn't do it for nearly long enough. It's no surprise that so many people still say how much they miss him. It's still hard to grasp how we can get by without him.

William Melvin Hicks was born in Georgia. He moved to Houston at the age of seven. By the time he was 13, he was writing and performing comedy. His first public gig was in the unlikely setting of a Baptist summer camp. He first got noticed as a member of a Houston-based outfit called the Outlaws Of Comedy. He remained an outlaw all his life. In this story, though, the outlaw turned out to be the good guy. Stand-up comedy, he declared, is the last bastion of free speech: 'I'm just waiting for someone to tell me I can't talk about a subject.'

Bill Hicks died of pancreatic cancer in February 1994 at the age of 32.

16
Jim Driver

...rants on about 'Situation Comedies' (both good and bad) and picks some prime examples

N ever trust a television executive to know funny from a hole in the head. Believe it: these guys have no sense of humour and never laugh at anything they haven't produced. Their only concerns are 'conflict', 'character building and development'. And that's why, for every *Fawlty Towers*, *One Foot In the Grave* or *Police Squad* made, there are twenty unfunny 'sit-com' soaps like *Bread*, *Solo* and *Don't Wait Up*, all with less laughs per hour than the average edition of *Newsnight*.

It's just like drama producers who insist on telling us about their characters' home lives. Inevitably this will involve a rebellious teenager, an affair with the spouse's best friend and/or a drink problem. Don't they realise that whenever this sort of nonsense interrupts a fairly-decent plot, all over Britain a million kettles are turned on and a billion gallons of water are flushed through our loos in protest? We watch a detective programme to watch them detecting, not to find out whether Mike Burden's daughter has passed her bloody A-levels, or whether Taggart's wife has oiled her wheelchair recently. We watch sit-coms to laugh. Or at least, that used to be the idea.

When we watch *Fawlty Towers*, all we ever know or want to know about Basil is that he is a short-tempered, manic-depressive snob. We don't care what sort of childhood he had, or what his job was before he opened the hotel – and thankfully we are never told. If anyone other than John Cleese had taken the *Fawlty Towers* pilot script to the BBC, it would have been rejected out of hand and a 'depressingly-frank' letter sent back saying something like: 'I didn't feel I could associate with, or care about, the characters... there is no depth to them... you should consider each character's background, attitudes and relationships to others...' Absolute bollocks. We can do without another *You Rang, M'Lord?*, thank you very much.

Of course the characters *are* the most important part of any sit-com. Practically all the laughs in *Dad's Army* come from knowing about the people involved and how they will react to a given circumstance. But we don't need to know that Captain Mainwaring liked to dress up in his wife's knickers, or that Corporal Jones was secretly depressed about getting old, or that Private Godfrey was a secret member of the Black Shirts – even if they were true. We are told as much as we needed to know for comedy reasons. Even Corporal Wilson's relationship with Mrs Pike was only ever hinted at in 81 TV episodes, until the feature film came along, filled in a few gaps, and blew away a huge chunk of the joke.

Steptoe and Son was totally character-led: every episode a cunning battle of wits between the two main protagonists, but every jibe moved towards a laugh. Compare that to something like *Bread*, obsessed with its character's background and its own obsessions, but not very concerned about the comedy. Look at *Absolutely Fabulous*, a pastiche on the media world that has about as much depth to its characters as an extra-thin cigarette paper, whilst still managing to be very funny. Nevertheless, had anyone other than Jennifer Saunders taken it to the Beeb, it is very doubtful that we'd ever have seen it.

Comedies are often rejected on the grounds of being *too* funny. Really. More scripts are weeded out for having too many jokes in them than for being 'not funny'. You've only got to switch on the TV any night to see examples of the latter category. In Britain a 'comedy' can be almost totally humour-less, just so long as it has solid, rounded characters and a good storyline. There is little doubt that *Cheers* would have had most of its one-liners extracted if it had been made by the BBC instead of NBC. And don't get the idea I'm unfairly picking on the Beeb. ITV hardly puts in any effort at all. The best it can come up with for the '90s was nicked from BBC Radio.

There follows is a list of the funniest (and unfunniest) sit-coms of the last thirty-odd years. I stick purely to situation comedies. Equally wonderful comedy-dramas (such as *The Riff-Raff Element*, *Auf Wiedersehen, Pet*, and *Minder*) and sketch shows (like Milligan's brilliant *Q5* and *Q6*, *Not the Nine O'Clock News*, etc) have been rejected on the grounds of not fitting in.

Absolutely Fabulous (BBC; 1992-95)

Series one neatly followed the end of Thatcher, the demise of lager-louts and the resulting rejection of '80s barrow-boy morality, and *AbFab* became the first comedy smash hit of the '90s. Media types recognised the person sitting at the desk next to them, rushed to write about this wonderful pastiche of their glamorous world. None of them apparently noticed that the person next to them was doing exactly the same.

Jennifer Saunders wrote the scripts and played Edina, a hip if somewhat hippy, PR woman who said 'darling' every other word, drank champagne like tea and refused to admit middle age into her insecure but moneyed world. Julia Sawalha played her sensible, hard-working daughter Saffron, and June Whitfield Mother, but the real star of the piece was Joanna Lumley, right-on-reincarnate as the chain-smoking, ageing juvenile, fashion editor Patsy. Series two failed to move much further forward, and (as we go to press) Saunders is vowing that series three will be positively the last.

The Addams Family *(ABC; 1964-66)*

Black comedy based around the cartoons of Charles Addams and rather more stylish than CBS's rival *Munsters*, which shadowed its run on the rival network. Like several other family TV favourites of the time, the real star of the piece was a hand, in this case called Thing – played, incidentally, by Lurch actor Ted Cassidy. But unlike its fellow 'hands' Sooty and Rag, Tag and Bobtail, Thing performed without clothes or sartorial assistance of any kind. Uncle Fester was played by former child actor Jackie Coogan, who had appeared as the title character opposite a certain Charles Chaplin his film *The Kid* in 1921. What he did between pre-pubescent boyish glory and aged ugliness is unclear.

All Gas and Gaiters *(BBC; 1967-71)*

The best in a long line of ecclesiastical comedies that includes *Our Man at St Mark's* (with Donald Sinden as the vicar with a cassock in his mouth), *Oh Brother!*, *Oh Father!* and *Hell's Bells* – the last three starring semi-professional cleric Derek Nimmo. In *All Gas and...* Nimmo played gormless Mervyn Noote (crazy name, not so crazy kind of guy), chaplain to the Bishop of St Oggs (William Mervyn). Also on hand 'to help with the fun' were John Barron as the puritanical Dean, and veteran British farce actor Robertson Hare as the fun-loving, if somewhat ancient, Archdeacon.

Most of the action (as there was) centred around the Dean's attempts to spoil the Bishop and Archdeacon's fun, and Noote's unwitting resolution of the problem. Towards the end of the run the aged Robertson Hare started to forget his lines and part of the programme's appeal was to watch the look of absolute horror develop on the other character's faces as he did so. Like so many enduring comedies of the '60s, *All Gas and Gaiters* began life as a *Comedy Playhouse* presentation called 'The

Bishop Rides Again'. Now, why don't they bring this idea back? It's not as though we're overwhelmed by brilliant sit-coms, is it?

'Allo 'Allo (BBC; 1984-92)

Perhaps Jeremy Lloyd and David Croft should have thought a little harder before launching this pastiche on the adventures of the wartime French Resistance. In it we don't see any Jews, gypsies, disabled people (or anybody else for that matter) getting tortured or sent to the Nazi death camps by the jovial German soldiers, and even The Gestapo (as represented by Herr Flick and Von Smallhausen) are more concerned with recovering giant sausages than they are with killing opponents of their fascist regime. Maybe Croft and Lloyd should write a sit-com based on *The Diaries of Anne Frank*. It could even be shorter on laughs than this repetitive, xenophobic nonsense.

Barney Miller (ABC, US; 1975-82)

Vastly underrated comic counterpart to *Hill Street Blues* in which the amiable but accomplished Captain Miller (Hal Linden) presided over the multi-cultural squad of detectives at New York's 12th Precinct. Like so many successful comedies, the action was restricted to a small number of sets (in this case, just the squadroom and Barney's office) and the comedy had to come from the characters and from the situation. Among the regulars were laconic Det Phil Fish (Abe Vigoda, who starred as one of the Mafia henchmen in *The Godfather*), simple but athletic and honourable Det Wojohowicz (Max Gail), gambler and general lead-swinger Det Yemana (Jack Soo) and ambitious dry-as-dust black Det Harris (Ron Glass).

The Beverly Hillbillies (CBS, US; 1962-71)

Starring Buddy Ebsen as Jed Clampett, the premise of this hugely popular sit-com was that a simple rural family strike oil on their poor Ozark Mountain small-holding and head off to start a new life in Beverly Hills on the proceeds. Seen by some as an attack on materialism, it was actually more of a piss-take of poor, simple country people. The episode broadcast in America on January 8th, 1964 recorded one of the biggest audiences ever. Forty-four million people tuned in to see the Clampetts have their vittles cooked for them by the Beverly Caterers, who they assumed (in their simple, country way), must be an old 'widder-woman' called Beverly trying to scrape a living after her man had died...

Bewitched *(ABC, US; 1964-72)*

It starred Elizabeth Montgomery (daughter of actor, Robert), in what was basically a one-joke situation. White witch Samantha (Montgomery) is forbidden by her husband Darrin (Dick York, after '69 Dick Sargent) from practicing witchcraft. Darrin is hardly a New Man: although he regularly brings home his advertising clients to dinner and expects his wife Samantha to cook for them and entertain them, he forbids her to use simple spells, insisting instead that she do all the washing and cleaning by hand. As Isaac Asimov remarked at the time: 'here's a woman with unimaginable magic power and she uses it entirely to shore up her husband's ego.'

At first only Samantha and her mother, Endora (Agnes Moorehead) were able to to do the magic, but as the series ran out of ideas, other magical characters (including Aunt Clara, the supernatural Dr Bombay and Sam's two eventual children, Tabitha and Adam) were brought in, and time travel became a regular occurrence. In one episode Samantha's twin sister Serena (played by Montgomery in a mini-skirt and beads) is arrested at a 'hippie (sic) love-in'. Needless to say, Darrin thinks it is Samantha (he doesn't know of Serena's existence) and even conservative Sam is embarrassed by her 'weirdo' sister. Other episodes featured Queen Victoria, Napoleon, Prince Charming and the Loch Ness Monster. All in all, it ran for eight years and notched up 252 episodes.

Blackadder *(BBC; 1983-89)*

Beginning pretty feebly in the 15th Century as plain old *Black*

Adder, this historical sit-com moved steadily through the ages, getting funnier and funnier all the time. *Blackadder II* (Elizabethan), led to *Blackadder the Third* (Regency) until we reached the far more assured *Blackadder Goes Forth*, set in the trenches of the First World War. Its regular stars, Rowan Atkinson in the title role, and Tony Robinson as his servant Baldrick, were joined by a succession of 'Alternative' comedians in guest roles, including Peter Cook as Richard III, Robbie Coltrane as Dr Johnson and Geoffrey Palmer as Field Marshall Haig. It also led to co-writer and Emma Freud bedfellow Richard Curtis being allowed write the script for *Four Weddings and a Funeral*, and so make his fortune.

Bread *(BBC; 1986-91)*

Hard to believe that this most unfunny and self-conscious of British 'comedies' ran to 68 episodes before someone high up realised it had used up its laugh. For some unGodly reason – probably related to the one that makes *The Sun* the best-selling 'newspaper' in Britain and Michael Barrymore our 'most loved TV personality' – *Bread* was consistently voted the top comedy programme in the country. Yuk.

Brighton Belles *(Carlton; 1993-)*

You'd think that it would be difficult to have access to all the *Golden Girls* scripts and a cast as distinguished as Sheila Hancock, Sheila Gish, Wendy Craig and Jean Boht, *and* still make an absolute stinker, wouldn't you? But they did. You'd also have thought that all the abominations that resulted when the formats of British sit-coms were exported to the US would have warned them off, but no. When you're called Carlton TV, it appears that you have to learn by your own mistakes. The way they're going, they'll be the wisest TV company in the world.

Cheers *(NBC, US; 1982-93)*

Masterful sit-com set in a fictitious Boston bar owned by womanizing, alcoholic, former football star, Sam Malone, played with relish by a be-rugged Ted Danson. His staff included romantic egg-headed waitress Diane Chambers (Shelley Long), not so romantic, but rougher and readier waitress Carla Tortelli (Rhea Pearlman), and punch-drunk barman Coach (Nick Colasanto). The mutually-denied attraction between Sam and Diane eventually blossomed in to a stormy on-off relationship, before Shelly Long escaped the series by means of getting Diane to jilt Sam at the altar. He went off on a world cruise, and (heart-mended) he returned to find the darkly attractive Rebecca How (Kirstie Alley) managing the bar.

Colasanto died in 1984 and Coach was replaced behind the bar by naive backwoods yokel Woody Boyd, played by future *Natural Born Killers* star, Woody Harrelson. The customers included barfly and sometime accountant Norm (George Wendt), middle-aged bachelor postman Cliff (John Ratzenburger) and suave but insecure psychiatrist Frasier Crane (Kelsey Grammer). Cheers is doubly notable in sit-com land for being (a) funny, and (b) one of the first sit-coms to successfully use a running story-line in addition to a self-contained weekly story. This, coupled with some bright and witty writing and the superb character-acting, kept *Cheers* at the top of the US ratings for four seasons Hopefully Carlton will do a British version starring Paul Shane as Sam, Molly Sugden as Diane and Richard O'Sullivan as Frasier.

Dad's Army *(BBC; 1968-77)*

It's hard to believe that Jimmy Perry and David Croft later went on to create such shabby articles as *It Ain't Half Hot Mum*, *'Allo 'Allo*, and *You Rang, M'Lord*. This wonderfully conceived and beautifully executed sit-com was their first joint venture in comedy and came out of their own (individual) experiences in the British Home Guard. Part of the secret of the show's success was in the casting of the Walmington-on-Sea platoon: Arthur Lowe as stuffy and snobbish bank manager Captain Mainwaring, John Le Mesurier as former public schoolboy bank clerk Wilson, John Laurie as the doom-obsessed undertaker Private Frazer, Clive Dunn as alarmist old-fogey and butcher Corporal Jones, Arnold Ridley (writer of *Ghost Train*) as conscientious objector Godfrey, Ian Lavender as the young and naive Pike, with James Beck playing the good-hearted spiv, Walker. Not that we should forget Bill Pertwee as the 'common' greengrocer/head Air Raid Warden, Frank Williams as the vicar and Edward Sinclair as the verger.

    Dad's Army was pretty safe ground for the two writers. Perry had been a 17-year old home guard private like Pike (his father even used to call him 'stupid boy') and Croft had served as a young ARP warden, but he insists, 'very unlike Hodges'. The central relationship was between the grammar school-educated Mainwaring – who had pulled himself up by his bootstrings – and 'privileged' former public schoolboy Wilson. It was a tremendous source of satisfaction to Mainwaring that he should have been Wilson's superior at both the bank and in the home guard. But Wilson was enough of a rebel not to care. A spin-off series centred around Arthur Wilson's promotion to bank manager is best left forgotten, and unnamed…

Dick Van Dyke Show (CBS, US; 1961-66)

Originally conceived by game show host and writer Carl Reiner as his own starring vehicle, this archetypal sit-com was called *Head of the Family* for its pilot episode. Johnny Carson was favourite to play the part of Rob Petrie, but – as we all know – former Illinois advertising executive, song and dance man and bit part actor (whose most notable part up until then was as Bilko's hillbilly cousin in *The Phil Silvers Show*) Dick Van Dyke pipped Carson at the post. Part of the reason for the casting was that Mel Brooks associate Reiner was thought to look 'too Jewish' for a prime time sit-com lead. The comedy was split between Rob's home – which he shared with his delectable ex-dancer wife Laura (played with considerable aplomb by Mary Tyler Moore, who went on to become a major sit-com player in her own right) and son Ritchie – and the office, where Petrie worked as scriptwriter on the 'Alan Brady Show'. Reiner was however allowed to play the part of Brady whenever he made one of his all-too infrequent screen appearances, but we were only ever shown the back of his head.

Doctor Down Under *(Australian TV; 1980)*

After a spiralling series of interminable *Doctor…* sit-coms based originally on the books of Richard Gordon – *Doctor in the House, Doctor at Large, Doctor in Charge, Doctor at Sea, Doctor on the Go, Doctor Without a Laugh in Sight* – some bright spark had the idea of transporting Doctors Duncan Waring (Robin Nedwell) and Dick Stuart-Clarke (Geoffrey Davies) out to Australia for a further series of 13 episodes (as if 147 set at St Swithins and environs weren't plenty). The laughs were even thinner on the ground in Australia than they had been in England, despite a fair amount of recycling and some routine attacks on 'whinging poms'. Just when we thought that this disastrous romp had seen off the Doctors for good, the same team re-emerged in 1991 (on the BBC this time, LWT having shown uncharacteristic good taste) as middle-aged fat-cats in the ill-advised *Doctor at the Top*. Let's just hope there won't be any more follow-ups. *Doctor in the Shroud*, perhaps?

Drop The Dead Donkey *(Channel 4; 1990-)*

Andy Hamilton and Guy Jenkin's TV newsroom romp has been Channel 4's only commissioned sit-com triumph to date, and perhaps if there had been a touch more opposition, it might not have won the several mantelpiece's worth of awards it has. Funny, but not often hilarious, the programme's success lies partly in the innovative way it reacts to current news stories – a bit of a downer, when it comes to repeats – and partly as a normal character-led sit-com. But the writing's good (if occasionally on the lines of newspaper cartoon punchlines) and the acting a cut above. Not an essential part of the viewing week, but funnier – and often more informative – than *News at Ten*.

Ever Decreasing Circles (BBC; 1984-89)

Underestimated comedy in which British sit-com stalwart Richard Briers played Martin Bryce, a pathetically insecure character who insisted on running his life (as well as everyone else's) with clockwork efficiency. The finely-tuned scripts from John Esmonde and Bob Larbey ensured that Martin's organisational blunders and the obvious attraction between wife Ann (Penelope Wilton) and easy-going smoothy neighbour Paul (Peter Egan) kept up a constant source of humour and story satisfaction. It finished its final run in full creative flow, as all good sit-coms should.

Fall & Rise of Reginald Perrin (BBC; 1976-79)

David Nobb's finest (half) hours to date, with the eponymous Reginald Iolanthe Perrin played with consummate skill by the late Leonard Rossiter. The eccentricity of the characters at Sunshine Deserts – including John Baron as boss CJ and John Horsley as Doc Morrisey – and at home – most notably Geoffrey Palmer as brother-in-law Jimmy and Leslie Schofield as boring estate agent son-in-law Tom – are amplified through Reggie's eyes. He has a breakdown, fakes his own suicide and returns to wife Elizabeth (Pauline Yates) as Reggie's old friend Martin Welbourne. The putrid American version, *Reggie*, starring Richard Mulligan, should be avoided at all costs.

Fawlty Towers (BBC; 1975-79)

Possibly the funniest six hours ever put down on videotape, *Fawlty Towers* was immaculately scripted by Cleese and his then-wife and co-star, Connie Booth, who blithely disregarded every so-called 'rule' of comedy. From Fawlty's first appearance fawning to the bogus Lord Melbury in 'A Touch of Class' to his final scene being dragged by his heels from the dining room by Manuel (Andrew Sachs) at the end of 'Basil The Rat', we learn absolutely nothing about him other than that he was a snobbish, puritanical Torquay hotel-keeper with a barely-concealed power complex, a foul, unpredictable temper and a wife (played by the wonderful Prunella Scales) he doesn't quite understand. But do we need to know any more?

The Gnomes Of Dulwich (BBC; 1969)

Jimmy Perry again. Our Jim had a brilliant idea: team Terry Scott and Hugh Lloyd (fresh from their long-running success in *Hugh and I*) with John Clive, dress them up as British-crafted stone garden gnomes, and put them in to a studio-garden next to one occupied by some cheap plastic gnomes that are – horror of horrors – mass-produced by *foreigners*. Can't think how it could have failed.

The Golden Girls (NBC, US; 1986-93)

Four old women living in retirement may not be the most promising theme for a sit-com, but Rue McClanahan, Betty White, Bea Arthur and Estelle Getty breathed added life in to some already powerful and witty scripts. Creator Susan Harris (of *Soap* fame) hit on an unlikely but rich comedic vein but refused to compromise when it came to tough subjects. In the last series Dorothy falls victim to an unknown illness, and is convinced that she has cancer, a tumour, or something worse. Death made regular visits to Blanche's Florida home as did the subjects of infertility, loneliness and sex. There was quite a lot about sex with Blanche around. The humour was usually quirky and often totally unpredictable. For example:

SOPHIA: My arthritis is bothering me, my social security cheque is late and I realised I haven't showered with a man for 22 years.

DOROTHY: Ma, pop's been dead 27 years.

SOPHIA: What's your point?

ROSE: Isn't it obvious? She showered with a dead man for five years.

Hancock's Half Hour (BBC; 1956-61)

Life at 23 Railway Cuttings, East Cheam, was often dull, usually down-at-heel, but inevitably funny. The Hancock/Sid James team that transferred from radio was too much of a partnership for Hancock to allow to continue, and Sid was duly written out for the last BBC series. Funnily, this is the series people remember most, as Anthony Aloysius Hancock – no longer resident in Cheam, but surrounded by 'real' actors like Patrick Cargill, June Whitfield and Hugh Lloyd – played a slightly less seedy version of himself in 'The Bedsitter', 'The Bowmans', 'The Radio Ham', 'The Lift', 'The Blood Donor' and 'The Succession – Son and Heir'.

Then Hancock ditched writers Galton and Simpson and moved to ATV to perform in a series of 13 playlets. These included another variant of the 'Hancock' character working a department store assistant for a bet (in a story written by Lord Charles' mate Ray Alan), other stories involved him working as a male escort to an Australian millionairess, and as comedy scriptwriter to 'great comedian' Francis Matthews. My, how the heart yearned for days of East Cheam and roses.

It is also worth pointing out that Hancock's great feature film was *The Punch and Judy Man*, which contains far more of what Hancock was about than the earlier *Rebel*. Despite the appalling bun fight and the woefully inadequate direction by Jeremy Summers (a rising young TV director who went on to direct the appalling *Ferry Across The Mersey*), *The Punch and Judy Man* contains some fine set-pieces. Especially the breakfast scene in which it is obvious that Hancock's character Wally and his wife Delia (Sylvia Syms) don't get on, and the ice cream-eating scene where Hancock learns technique from the young boy. The film also contains one of the best ever performances from John Le Mesurier as Wally's friend, The Sandman. So there.

Happy Ever After/Terry & June (BBC; 1974-78/1979-87)
First as the Fletchers and then as the Medfords, Terry Scott and June Whitfield played basically the same middle-class suburban couple for over 110 episodes through 13 years. Whether they were having their quite gentle misunderstandings with

the vicar, the dipsomaniac Aunt Lucy, or with Terry's unreasonable boss Sir Dennis, the jokes were equally mild and the tar-
gets well-padded. Although lambasted in hindsight by most of
today's TV executives, writers, performers and critics as being
just too cosy and out of step with reality, a consistently funny
(admittedly in quite a gentle way) sit-com like this might go
down quite well at White City in these barren times.

I Love Lucy/The Lucy Show (CBS, US; 1951-'61/1962-68)

In the archetypal sit-com, I Love Lucy, Hollywood veteran Lucille Ball played Lucy Ricardo, wife of Cuban bandleader
Ricky Ricardo (played by her real-life husband and real-life
Cuban bandleader Desi Arnaz). Most plots centred around
Lucy trying to relieve her drab housewife existence and join in
with Ricky's showbusiness life-style, which for some unex-
plained reason he didn't want her to do. Their landlords and
next-door neighbours, Ethel and Fred Mertze (played by Vivian
Vance and William Frawley), were a retired vaudeville couple
who could usually be relied on to help Lucy in her endeavours.

After her divorce from Desi Arnaz, Lucy hitched up
with new producer husband Gary Morton for a series set in
Connecticut (later transferred to California), featuring two new
children Chris and Jerry, flat-mate Vivian (Vivian Vance again)
and new bosses at the bank where she worked (loose description), first played by Dick Martin – of Laugh In fame – and later,
and somewhat more memorably, by Gale Gordon. It was twaddle, but usually quite funny twaddle.

Last Of The Summer Wine (BBC; 1973-)

Over a soundtrack of maudlin' harmonica music, a group of
old codgers tramp around a quite picturesque Yorkshire land-
scape, delivering repetitive speeches to each other and to a succession of grey-haired women in curlers. It was quite funny
once upon a time, but after almost 150 episodes, it's difficult to
remember when – or why. All those involved (including writer
Roy Clarke) are old enough to know better.

The Likely Lads/Whatever Happened to...BBC; 1964-66/ 1973-74)

It's not often a sequel betters the original, but that's just what happened here. Originally a sit-com about two girl-obsessed teenage lads working in an electronics factory in Newcastle-upon-Tyne, Dick Clement and Ian La Frenais' *Likely Lads* could have been written with *Whatever Happened to the...* in mind. Terry (James Bolam) was the feckless one, keen to take risks and with no thought of tomorrow, whereas Bob (Rodney Bewes) was already making plans, and clearly had the rude beginnings of ambition stabbing away at his insides.

Whatever Happened to the... began seven years after we thought we'd said goodbye to the 22-year old Lads, and in the intervening years Bob had struggled to 'better himself' and escape from his working-class shackles. He is engaged to the socially-climbing Thelma and they are about to get married and buy a house of their own. His alter-ego Terry, on the other hand, has spent too much time in the army, married a 'bit of German crumpet' and returned to his working class Newcastle roots, a more stoic (but not too much wiser) man. The main battles are between Thelma and Terry for Bob's soul and between Bob and Terry as childhood rivals.

Man About The House (Thames; 1973-75)

Three young(ish) people sharing a flat: two female and one male. Hard to believe that this was an idea considered riské at the time (more so in Cheltenham than Chelsea, methinks) and Richard O'Sullivan (Robin), Paula Willcox (Chrissy) and Sally Thomsett (Jo) milked John Esmonde and Bob Larbey's scripts for all they were worth. Their landlords were the Ropers – played by Yootha Joyce and Brian Murphy – and the spin offs from this series became quite an industry for Thames TV. Although he was supposed to marry Chrissy in the final series, Tripp flies off to run the *Robin's Nest* bistro with Tony Blackburn's wife Tessa Wyatt, and the Ropers end up next door to the Fourmiles (including Shiela Fearn, who played Terry's sister in *The Likely Lads*) in suburban Hampton Wick in the series *George and Mildred*.

Marriage Lines *(BBC; 1963-66)*

A pretty sick-making affair today, but at the time quite a ground-breaking domestic sit-com written by Richard Waring and starring Richard Briers and Prunella Scales as young married couple George and Kate Starling. The main source of the comedy was all those little domestic problems other sit-coms have latched on to ever since. It may have been naive, middle-class twaddle, but at least it was naive British middle-class twaddle.

Me Mammy *(BBC; 1969-71)*

Hot shot middle-aged bachelor Bunjy (Milo O'Shea) has everything going for him. He is a top jet-setting executive, with a flash sports car, a luxury flat in Regent's Park and… a possessive mother. If the very idea makes you cringe, you should have seen all 11 hours of it.

Mr Ed *(syndicated/CBS, US; 1961-65)*

The subject is a talking horse, an idea nicked from the *Francis (The Talking Mule)* film series, by the movies' first director, Arthur Lubin, no less. As is the custom with this kind of phenomenon sit-com (other examples include *My Mother, The Car; My Favourite Martian, I Dream Of Jeannie*, etc), only one person is ever allowed access to the object of wonder. In this case, it is Alan Young's character Wilbur, and much of the situation humour comes from his trying to convince people that he's not gone mad. Another convention is that the horse/car/Martian/genie has to be cleverer than the person he/she is talking to. And this certainly is the case here: not only is Ed an avid reader (which puts him one step above Wilbur for a start), he is also appreciative of Beethoven, Mozart and Chopin and knows a bit about gourmet fodder. Wilbur's tastes stretched as far as 'popular dance music' and hamburgers.

My Mother, the Car (NBC, US; 1965-66)

It was a totally ludicrous idea in the first place, but the run-away success of *Mr Ed* in the early '60s, led to every possible avenue of 'magical' sit-com being exploited, from *Bewitched* to *My Favourite Martian* to *I Dream Of Jeannie* to *My Mother, the Car*. In this most cringe-making of cringe-makers, Dick Van Dyke's brother Jerry starred as car-freak lawyer Dave, whose dead mother is 'rein-car-nated' as a 1928 Porter sedan. She gives him advice (in the voice of Ann Sothern) over the car's radio and makes demands for garish new seat covers and assorted vehic-ular trinkets. It finally ended up in the scrap yard after 26 episodes. (If you ask him very, very nicely, Mark Lamarr might even sing you the show's theme song.)

The Munsters (CBS, US: 1964-66)

As in The Addams Family, the theme here is of a family of innocent 'horror characters' trying to live a decent life amidst a community of intolerant and unsympathetic 'normal' people. Herman (played by 6'7" Fred Gwynne) is based on Frankenstein's monster and works as a funeral director for Gateman, Goodbury and Graves. His wife Lily (Yvonne de Carlo) and Grandpa (Al Lewis, Gwynne's sidekick from *Car 54, Where Are You?*) are vampires, whilst son, Eddie (Butch Patrick) is a werewolf. Poor niece Marilyn (Pat Priest) is terrifyingly normal. The late follow-up, *The Munsters Today*, produced from 1989, uses the same characters (different actors) and pretty much the same gags, but somehow manages to avoid most of the humour.

Nearest And Dearest (Granada; 1968-72)

Largely forgotten Northern working-class comedy starring Jimmy Jewel and Hilda Baker as Eli and Nellie Pledge, joint inheritors of a near-bankrupt Lancashire pickle factory, Pledge's Pickles. Set-pieces like Baker's 'it's twenty-five past something... ooh, I really must get a second-hand put on this watch' and 'has he been?', as well as the immaculate comic-timing shown by this pair of music hall veterans meant that they were usually better even than the above-average scripts.

Never The Twain (Thames; 1981-91)

If Donald Sinden and Windsor Davies got paid on the level of their over-acting, they'd never have to work again. Their roles as feuding antique dealers, Oliver Smallbridge and Simon Peel might easily have turned them into sit-com superstars, but after a promising (if somewhat kitsch start) the romp soon petered out, largely thanks to Johnnie Mortimer's tired and often formulated scripts. All concerned went through the motions for a total of 69 episodes.

Not On Your Nellie (LWT; 1974-77)

Despite her spirited and well-cast performance opposite Jimmy Jewel in the naughty but nice *Nearest and Dearest*, veteran music hall 'turn' Hilda Baker was like a fish out of parsley sauce in this London-based comic vehicle. She starred as a teetotal Bolton lass who comes down south to help her womanizing, drunken gambler of a father (John Barrett) run his ramshackle Fulham boozer. Best left forgotten.

One Foot In The Grave (BBC; 1990-)

David Renwick's fresh and blackly-edged comedy centres around cantankerous retired security guard Victor Meldrew (Richard Wilson). It occasionally teeters into self-parody (a few too many 'I don't believe it's, and '...I'll be bound') creep in for totally comfortable viewing, but is practically the only British sit-com of the '90s that has (so far) never failed to satisfy.

Only Fools and Horses (BBC; 1981-93?)

Peckham is as unlikely a setting as writer John Sullivan's previous outing to Tooting in *Citizen Smith*, although most of the location shots were filmed in the Bristol area so as to get that genuine cockney feel. Del Boy (David Jason) is the scheming wide-boy head of the family who works to protect his better-educated but thicker younger brother Rodney (Nicholas Lyndhurst) and Grandad/Uncle Albert (Leonard

Pearce/Buster Merryfield) from life's cruelties – though he's not averse to ripping them off, when it suits him. Later in the series the programme expanded to fill a 50-minute slot, saw Rodney married off to Cassandra and brought in a love interest for Del in the shape of ex-stripper Raquel. A follow-up series has never been ruled out.

On The Buses (LWT; 1969-73)

Another hugely popular sit-com from the other two Rons, Wolfe and Chesney. Reg Varney starred as Stan Butler, a middle-aged, compulsively-womanizing bachelor who lived with his old mum (Cicely Courtneidge/Doris Hare), ugly sister Olive (Anna Karen) and work-shy brother-in-law Arthur (Michael Robbins). Stan was a bus driver for the suburban Luxton Bus Co, and his work-mates included sex-mad conductor Jack (Bob Grant), miserable inspector 'Blakey' (played with gusto by Stephen Lewis) and an assortment of nondescript male drivers and mini-skirted 'dollybird' clippies.

A typical plot would have Jack swanning through the canteen pretending to be 'queer', Arthur eating Olive's mud-pack instead of blancmange, Stan pretending that his bus full of attractive shop-girls has 'broken down' at the cemetery-gates, Blakey shouting 'I 'ate you, Butler!' at least three times, and everybody saying 'mate' far more than necessary, so as to establish their working-class credentials. Aimed squarely at the lowest common denominator, in comparison it makes Bernard Manning appear positively Shakespearean.

Phil Silvers Show (Bilko) (CBS, US; 1955-59)

A smooth-talking con artist has been at the centre of many a successful comedy and Nat Hiken's creation, Master-Sergeant Ernest G Bilko (RA 15042699) is the grand-daddy of them all. Bilko's cat-and-mouse relationship with Fort Baxter commander Colonel Hall (played by real life bumbler Paul Ford) is never far from the humour, and although Bilko outsmarted his superior in practically all of the 142 episodes made, the writers ended the run with a win for the Colonel. The final scenes of the last ever episode show Hall and Captain Barker gloating over a TV screen, on which we can see Bilko and his 'gang' in the gaol. 'Wonderful show, isn't it, Barker?' says the Colonel, 'And the best part is: as long as I'm sponsor, it will never be cancelled.' We cut to the guardhouse where Bilko makes a face and announces, cartoon-style: 'Th, th, that's all, folks!'

Silvers went on to play a similar character to Bilko, a factory supervisor called Harry Grafton in *The New Phil Silvers Show*, and 30 episodes were made by CBS in 1963, before it bombed. Robbed of Bilko side-kicks of the calibre of Duane Doberman (Maurice Gosfield, who went on to become the voice of Benny in *Top Cat*), Mess Sergeant Rupert Ritzik (Joe E Ross), Private Sam Fender (Herbie Faye), Corporal Rocco Barbella (Hervey Lembeck) and Cpl Henshaw (Alan Melvyn), it had too much to live up to, and too little new plotting to erase the Fort Baxter memories. Award for the best ever Bilko episode is normally divided between episode 49, 'Bilko Gets Some Sleep' (in which the insomniac Bilko, troubled by a guilty conscience, gives up gambling and scheming, only to be encouraged back into 'sin' by a worried camp who can't sleep for trying to work out what he's up to) and episode 28, 'The Court Martial (AKA The Case Of Harry Speakup)' (in which Bilko defends Zippo the Chimp, who has accidentally been enrolled in to the army). This latter episode contains some of Silver's best ad-libs as he reacts to the chimp's unpredictable behaviour in the courtroom scene.

Please Sir/The Fenn Street Gang *(LWT; 1968-73)*
It wasn't too bad when John Alderton was around to play the idealistic young schoolmaster, Bernard Hedges (at least old-timers like Deryck Guyler as caretaker Norman Potter, Erik Chitty as Smithy, Richard Davies as Price, Joan Sanderson as Doris Ewell and Noel Howlett as the headmaster, were on hand to provide some well-timed comic moments), but once he'd left

for pastures less gormless, the shit really hit the screen. In *Please Sir*, his part was taken by Glyn ('Dave the barman' in *Minder*) Edwards as Mr Dix, followed by 'toff' David ffitchett-Brown (Richard Warwick), who even had to contend with a class of new characters even more stereotypical than the 5C Hedges had to teach.

Over on the *Fenn Street Gang*, which preceded the final Alderton-less series of *Please Sir*, Mr Hedges had left school at the same time as the original 5C. It wasn't a moment too soon: the actors playing Abbott, Duffy, Sharon, Denis, Maureen and Craven were already starting to grey around the temples and one or two were said to be auditioning for *Last Of The Summer Wine*. The first series of *Please Sir* was innovative and fresh – it even ran for 45 minutes instead of the usual 30 – but it quickly became formulative and eventually downright embarrassing. Derek Guyler was the only consistently good thing about the show and in the film spin-off he was given the only funny line:

> *Frankie Abbott's Mother (after seeing him off on a school trip):* They had to do away with my Fallopians after I gave birth to little Frankie, you know.
> *Norman Potter:* Oh. Kept jumping up on the pram, did they?

And that really was the best line in the film.

Police Squad *(ABC, US; 1982-83)*

Lieutenant Frank Drebin (Leslie Nielsen) was the straight-faced accident-prone crime-buster who only got the chance to wise-cracked through six episodes before the ABC Network pulled the plug on what was probably America's most innovative sit-com. It certainly didn't fit any of the stereotypes, and plot advancements were as likely to come out of a pun as from a deduction. But the story has a happy ending: the characters, cast and producers transferred the format to the big screen and made an absolute mint out of the subsequent *Naked Gun* series.

Porridge (BBC; 1974-77)

Dick Clement and Ian La Frenais must rank as the most consistently funny comedy writing team in the business. All right, so Ronnie Barker and the rest of the cast – including Richard Beckinsale as Godber, Fulton Mackay as the Chief Officer, and Brian Wilde as Mr Barraclough – were superb in their relative roles, but the scripts joined Barker as the real star of the piece. Limited to the confines of HM Prison Slade (and perhaps the film of the series suffered from having a little too much 'freedom of movement'), with an almost exclusively male cast, Clement and La Frenais picked at the bones of the characters and brought out every last drop of the natural humour of the situation. Not surprisingly, the follow-up, *Going Straight*, although head and shoulders above most sit-coms of the period, lacks the magic that elevated *Porridge* above the opposition. It's hard to believe that only 20 episodes of *Porridge* were ever made.

The Rag Trade (BBC; 1961-63)

Believe it or not, at the time, this was the sit-com everybody stayed in to watch, which is doubly ironic when you consider that the show's catch-phrase was 'everybody out!'. Written by Ronald Chesney and Ronald Wolfe (who later went on to create *On The Buses*), it followed the Sellers film, *I'm All Right, Jack* in showing management and work-force out to get all they can out of life, but hopefully at the other's expense. Peter Jones played the scheming boss of Fenner Fashions and Reg Varney was foreman Reg. On the 'other side' were Miriam Karlin as shop steward Paddy, and the workers included (at various times) Sheila Hancock, Esma Cannon, *Laugh-In* girl Judy Carne, and Barbara Windsor, with Irene Handl sometimes stepping in to play Reg's mother.

A dire(r) sequel on LWT (1977-78) featured Jones and Karlin joined by a totally new workforce including Anna Karen (repeating her brilliant role as 'Olive' from *On The Buses*) and the *Eastenders* actress said to be a sucker for a man in a Range Rover, Gillian Taylforth.

Red Dwarf *(BBC; 1988-93?)*

Originally conceived by writers Rob Grant and Doug Naylor (who also work under the amalgam 'Grant Naylor') as *'Steptoe and Son* in space on acid', the concept of a science fiction sit-com proved difficult to sell to the BBC. The reason, as TV producer Paul Jackson explained, was that sci-fi is expensive to produce, but always ends up looking cheap. So, the initial *Dwarf* pilot script was kept deliberately low key, which helped (in the tradition of *Porridge* and *Steptoe and Son*) bring out some fine comic moments.

The first outing for the story was in a 1983 script for the BBC radio show *Son Of Cliché*, called 'Dave Hollins – Space Cadet'. its star was Chris Barrie, who went on to play the holo-gram Rimmer in the TV series, with Craig Charles as Lister, Danny John-Jules as The Cat, David Ross/Robert Llewellyn as robot Kryton, and Norman Lovett/Hattie Hayridge as the computer, Holly. Before it was cast, 'Grant Naylor' reveal that their idea of Lister was more of as an English Christopher Lloyd, with the Rimmer character played by a sort of 'English Dan Aykroyd'.

Reluctant Romeo *(BBC; 1966-67)*

What about a sit-com concerned with Leslie Crowther who has to fight off hordes of women – including Amanda Barrie, *Coronation Street*'s Alma Baldwin – because they find him *tooo* irresistible for words?

Rising Damp *(Yorkshire TV; 1974-78)*

A combination of a well-judged situation, great acting (Leonard Rossiter, Frances de la Tour, Richard Beckinsale and Don Warrington) and Eric Chappell's often superb – but never less than wonderful – scripts made for one of British comedy's finest moments. The 'action' rarely left the bedsits and landing in Rigsby's seedy house, and, as in *Porridge, Steptoe and Son* and

Cheers, this restricted atmosphere brings out some great character-led comedy. Only 28 episodes were ever made.

Roots *(ATV; 1981)*

Early Marks and Gran vehicle about a Jewish dentist (that's the best joke out of the way) played by Allan Corduner, who feels the need to give up his career in order to pursue his art. At least Lesley Joseph got the chance to try out a watered-down version of her *Birds of a Feather* Dorien character.

Roseanne *(US; 1988-)*

Ground-breaking blue-collar comedy set in small town Illinois, where decent folks may not always be right, but boy, do they try too hard. John Goodman's hard-working Dan usually plays second-fiddle to his domineering wife (Roseanne Barr/Arnold), who has normally worked out what they should do long before he gets home from work. The subjects covered include bringing up children without much – or any – money (the perennial theme), abortion, drugs, homelessness, unemployment and eating. Though since executive producer Barr/Arnold lost a few pounds, the subject of food has dropped down the comedy scale.

Soap *(ABC, US; 1977-81)*

Anarchic American sit-com that explored totally new territory in chronicling the saga of two American families, the Campbells and the Tates. This included a daughter who seduced a catholic priest, a woman who habitually slept with her mother's lovers and Benson, the butler who only did things when he wanted to do them. But every innovation was viciously fought for. According to *The Book Of Lists 2*, when *Soap* was first aired in the States, ABC executives decreed that the following changes be made: a 'positive Italian-American character' had to be present whenever the Mafia was mentioned in order to 'balance the negative stereotype'; references to CIA involvement in opium smuggling had to be cut; comments about Sun Myung Moon were banned; and there was some concern about using the name of Campbell, in case it should offend the Campbell Soup Company.

Solo (BBC; 1981-82)

Another unfunny comedy from Carla Lane, this one getting slightly fewer laughs than *Macbeth*. After being betrayed by her live-in boyfriend, Felicity Kendal realises she doesn't need a man in her life any more, and sets about going it alone. Fine, but did we need to watch her doing it?

Some Mothers Do 'Ave 'Em (BBC; 1973-78)

Lambasted by the critics at the time and since, for being simply gormless, *Some Mothers...* has the twin advantage of (a) the hair-raising (and often dangerous) stunts performed by star Michael Crawford in his role as the much-mimicked Frank Spencer, and (b)... being very funny.

Steptoe & Son (BBC; 1962-74)

Galton and Simpson were at the height of their writing powers, and obviously relished the luxury of being in charge and writing for real actors, after their long and increasingly-difficult relationship with Hancock. Wilfred Brambell and Harry H Corbett excelled in their roles as the father and son rag and bone merchants, skillfully squeezing out every last drop of malice from the claustrophobic love-hate relationship.

The superb casting was no accident: Galton and Simpson requested Corbett and Brambell specifically for the parts in the original *Comedy Playhouse* one-off, 'The Offer'. Both were highly-respected 'straight actors' – when the call came through, Mancunian Corbett was playing the title role in *Henry IV* and Dublin-born Brambell was starring on the west end stage – and there was genuine doubt as to whether the parts would be considered beneath them. Luckily, they decided to give it a go.

The central premise was that middle-aged Harold could feel his life slipping away from him, and week after week he sought to rid himself of the old man's smothering influence.

But his every attempt was doomed to failure. All Harold had to do was walk out of the door and leave Oil Drum Lane forever, but he could never do it. Albert was an expert in lead-swinging and knew exactly how to wrap his son around his gnarled little fingers. If this involved deflating Harold's middle-class pretensions at the same time, all the better.

The series ran for a total of 57 episodes, with most of the action played out in the Steptoe's junk-ridden lounge. If there were any other actors involved, it was rarely more than one or two: one of Harold's girlfriends, perhaps (before the old man could put her off), a travel agent, or a visiting tax inspector. *Steptoe and Son* was at its best as a cat and mouse game between the two main characters. Every week, as Ron Grainger's *Old Ned* theme faded out at the start of the show, you knew instinctively that Albert was going to come out on top, but you hoped, just for once, that Harold might come out a winner. He never did.

Sykes *(BBC; 1960-80)*

Long-running and hugely popular sit-com (over 22 million viewers at its peak) teaming under-estimated writer and performer Eric Sykes with *Carry On...* and *Hancock* star Hattie Jacques as twin brother and sister 'Hat and Eric' of 24 Sebastopol Terrace. The first episode was subtitled *Sykes and a Telephone* and every week there'd be a new subject for them to tackle. Richard Wattis played the neighbour at various times, and towards the end of the run Deryck Guyler popped up as Corky, the friendly but pretty thick, local policeman. Sykes wrote the scripts (sometimes assisted by Johnny Speight) and managed to attract a few well-known guest stars, including a rather famous excursion with Peter Sellers.

Taxi *(ABC/NBC, US; 1978-83)*

You'd be hard-pressed to find a more rounded bunch of characters than those at New York's Sunshine Cab Company. Heartless controller Louis de Palma (Danny DeVito), warm and generous lead Alex Rieger (Judd Hirsch), well-meaning Latvian Latka Gravas (Andy Kaufman), the spaced out Reverend Jim Ignatowski (Christopher Lloyd), and struggling single-parent Elaine Nardo (Marilu Henner) among them. Created and scripted by the magic team of James L Brooks, Allen Burns and Grant Tinker, former MTM writers and producers on *The Mary Tyler Moore Show* and *Rhoda*.

Till Death Us Do Part/In Sickness And In Health (BBC; 1965-75/1985-92)

When it first hit the screens in 1965, Johnny Speight's working-class comedy caused genuine shock-waves around Britain. It then transferred to America for a watered-down version called *All in the Family* and did much the same thing there. As Milton Shulman wrote in 1968: 'the fascination of Alf Garnett... lay in his ability to act as a distorting mirror in which we could watch our meanest attributes reflected large and ugly.' Foul-mouthed Tory-voting, bigoted, monarchist Alf Garnett was originally intended by Speight to be a figure of ridicule, and his outrageous views were meant to be laughed at, rather than applauded. But, you can't keep the idiots down, and in public bars all over Britain Alf-clones appeared, proudly spouting the same kind of racist, right-wing non-logic as their 'hero'. Some even went on to write columns for *The Sun*.

Like practically all the good sit-coms of the time, *Till Death...* began life as a single one-off play in the *Comedy Playhouse* slot, but with the family name being Ramsay, and wife Else played by Gretchen Franklin, who ended up as Ethel in *Eastenders*. But by the time the series proper began in June 1966, Dandy Nichols was firmly in place as Else and the family name was Garnett. Daughter Rita was played by Una Stubbs and her layabout 'scouse-git' of a husband, Mike (meant to be Alf's Labour-voting political opposite) was played by Anthony Booth. The arguments were madly illogical affairs (usually brought down to earth by one of the two women) about race, football, God, sex and the royal family. Although he would never admit defeat, or even notice it, Alf usually lost – at least on moral grounds.

By the time the BBC got around to doing a follow-up in 1985, ATV had already attempted a revival called *Till Death...*, produced by William G Stewart of *15 To 1* and *The Price Is Right* fame. This best-forgotten seven-part series saw Alf and Else retired down to a house in Eastbourne with Patricia Hayes as their lodger, Min, and Rita as only an occasional visitor. Returning to the Beeb, Speight's wrote *In Sickness and in Health* partly as an attack on NHS and welfare state cuts. In the first series of *In Sickness and...* Else was confined to a wheelchair, and by the second she was dead. Alf's run-ins with his neighbour/fiance Mrs Hollingberry and with the gay, black social worker assigned to him, were all very well, but not a patch on the fire and strength of the original series.

Up The Elephant & Down The Castle *(Thames; 1983-85)*
The prospect of chirpy chappie Jim Davidson playing a character called Jim London, and inheriting a house in SE17 was bad enough, but throw in a few dodgy 'heart-of-gold' type cockney-type characters (including Christopher Ellison rehearsing for his DI Burnside role as best mate, Arnold) and the result was...

Very nearly as bad as the follow-up, *Home James*. For those who like their humour not so much sign-posted as with a motorcycle escort.

The Upchat Line *(Thames; 1977)*
Another totally sad idea, this time with John Alderton playing Mike Upchat, a writer with a compulsion for chatting-up every attractive woman he comes across, and who has his base at a left-luggage locker on Marylebone Station. Honest. An even worse follow-up, *The Upchat Connection*, starred Robin Nedwell. Even sadder is that the deviser and writer of both was none other than Keith Waterhouse.

Who Is Sylvia? (ATV; 1967)

After a successful stint in the title role of *The Worker*, roly-poly real-life womanizer Charlie Drake turned up again as a bachelor looking for a perfect mate through Mrs Proudpiece's marriage bureau. It really needed a Mr Pugh (Henry McGee) to save it, but he was too busy flogging Sugar Puffs in TV ads.

Whoops Apocalypse! (LWT; 1982)

You'd think that with a cast that included John Cleese, Richard Griffiths, Alexei Sayle, Geoffrey Palmer and with a script by David Renwick and Andrew Marshall, a sit-com like this couldn't possibly fail. But it did.

The Young Ones (BBC; 1982-84)

It was just a matter of time before TV got around to harnessing some of the new talent from the fledgling 'alternative' comedy circuit. Producer Paul Jackson was a regular on comedy gig guest-lists and had become as much a fixture at the Comedy Store and Comic Strip as compere Alexei Sayle. Written by Ben Elton, Rik Mayall and (his girlfriend/manager) Lise Mayer, *The Young Ones* starred Ade Edmondson as the unpredictably violent Vyvyan, Nigel Planer as sad hippy Neil, Rik Mayall was the silly sex-obsessed virgin Rick, and Christopher Ryan played the one no-one can remember (called Mike).

There wasn't much to do in the way of character development, because most of the characters had already been aired in some form or another on various stages around the capital. Alexei Sayle played the landlord Jerzy Balowski (whose name is an anagram of a well-known Liverpool comedian, no prizes for guessing who) as well as various members of his family, for which Sayle insisted on writing his own lines.

And plotting? What plotting? The plots that did creep through the net usually involved demolishing/blowing-up a wall/building/car and/or television set, as a means to involving a guest singer or band in a *Two Ronnies*-type musical interlude. But the music was far more likely to be supplied by The

Damned or John Otway than Elkie Brooks or Barbara Dickson. Special guest comedians included just about every performer who had ever set foot at the Store/Strip, from Lenny Henry, French and Saunders, Hale and Pace, to Fry and Laurie, Arnold Brown, Norman Lovett and Ben Elton. Adored by every teenager who didn't belong to a church youth club (plus one or two who did), and tolerated by everyone else because it was 'new', *The Young Ones* opened plenty of TV doors for a new type of comedian. Pity that trend hasn't been repeated since.

You Rang, M'Lord? (BBC; 1988-93)

Little more than an excuse to get the Perry/Croft repertory company of Donald Hewlett, Michael Knowles, Paul Shane, Su Pollard, Bill Pertwee and Jeffrey Holland off the dole for an extended skit on *Upstairs, Downstairs*. The set-pieces were more repetitive than funny and the plots as ludicrous and drawn-out as any to fly from the Perry/Croft typewriter in its twilight years. That the Bob Monkhouse-sung closing theme song was the best thing about this 26-episode travesty, says it all.

Yus My Dear (LWT; 1976)

It's the Two Rotten Rons again – Wolfe and Chesney – writers and creators of such classics as *On The Buses* and *The Rag Trade*, with yet another total stinker. Wally and Lily Briggs (played by those two thespians the RSC somehow missed, Arthur Mullard and Queenie Watts) were reasonably funny as supporting characters in the James Beck vehicle, *Romany Jones*, but move them out to a council flat of their own, team them up with Mike Reid and the results are truly terrible. The title (repeated at regular intervals by Mullard) was the funniest thing about the whole show.

17
Malcolm Hardee
...Attends 'Freddy Mercury's Birthday Party'

7th October 1986, 10.30am.

The phone rings.

I pick it up and answer with the usual 'Oy! Oy!'

'Hello, it's Louis here.' An agent. 'Are The Greatest Show On Legs still working?'

'Yup.'

'How do you fancy doing a show for Freddy Mercury's fortieth birthday?

'How much? How long? Where?'

'£600. Three-and-a-half minutes' Balloon Dance, Club Xenon, Piccadilly.'

'Okay. When?'

'Tomorrow night.'

So, we're booked to perform our infamous Balloon Dance for the lead singer of Queen's fortieth. (This is a routine I do with two other guys, consisting of us dancing stark naked – apart from strategically-placed balloons – to the tune of *Tea For Two [cha cha cha]*.) I ring the other two and they are as keen as mustard. Big Freddie Mercury fans both, and, after all, a hundred quid is a hundred quid!

8th October 1986, 8pm.

We arrive at Club Xenon, 171 Piccadilly, and are ushered

to the 'dressing room', which in reality is a cupboard behind the stage. There is, however, a small window in the door through which we can peer out across the stage at the celebrity party-goers. The Management inform us that we must remain in the cupboard until we have finished our set. There are four or five other acts, including a Russian acrobat and a midget.

The show begins. Freddie's in, so's Elton John, Princess Margaret and Rod Stewart. The party-goers ignore the first three acts, but the Russian acrobat goes down well. It's the midget's turn next. We'd been holding him up to the window to see what was going on, and fuelled by our recently acquired camaraderie, we watch while he goes through his midget routine.

Freddie's management – six blokes in funny suits and ties – come in to the cupboard and inform us that we can't go on. I'm naked and ready to go. Quite reasonably, I ask why. The Management tell me that our act might be considered 'gay'. The press are in and Freddie doesn't want to be considered 'gay'.

Obviously disappointed, I try to reason with them by pointing out that (1) it's obvious to anybody that Freddie Mercury is gay, (2) the band's name is Queen, for fuck's sake, and (3) what's the big deal, anyway? I peer through the window and notice Freddie with his tongue down Elton's throat. The Management will have none of it, and insist on paying me off in full. I would have put the £600 into my pocket, but as I was only wearing a sock at the time…

I'm disappointed and disillusioned, but what the hell: there's a party to go to. I ask the Management if we can get dressed and join in. 'After he's cut the cake,' they reply. Off they go, locking the door behind them. We then suffer the indignity of peering through a 10" x 8" window, waiting for the cake to arrive.

After about 15 minutes, it appears. It's huge: a great pink cake in the shape of a Rolls-Royce, complete with the number plates FM1. Three burly carriers lay it on three tables for Freddie to cut. He stands behind the cake, the paparazzi stand in front. Freddie grasps a 12" knife in both hands, and poses for pictures. He stabs the cake and strides off. The dressing-room door is finally unlocked and I ask the Management if we could please come out and join the party. One of them points and says that we can go into 'that bit' (the room in front of the stage), but not in to 'that bit' (an ante room containing Freddie, Rod, Princess, Elton, etc). We go into 'that bit' (in front of the stage).

'Our bit' is full of liggers and hangers-on paying £5 for pints of piss water, in the vain hope of meeting somebody famous. By now I am doubly disappointed. Not only have we not been allowed to perform, but we're not even allowed to meet anyone we were supposed to perform in front of. By this time it's 2am, and I suggest to the others that we fuck off home, especially as I've got to get up early with the kids. We head for a side door.

In the corridor by the exit – untouched except for a single stab wound – is Freddie Mercury's Birthday Cake. I look at my companions, they look at me, and I utter the words I know they want to hear:

'We'll have that,' I say.

You would never think a cake could weigh so much. We certainly don't, until we drag it out of the door and to our Ford Transit, which (as luck would have it) is parked a mere 20 yards away. We open the back and in it goes… well, not quite. There are still three or four feet sticking out of the back. And so we drive the eight miles back to my house in south-east London with the back end of Freddie Mercury's pink Roller sticking out of the back of our battered Transit.

We arrive back at my place only to discover that we can't get the thing up the stairs. Martin – the sensible Balloon Dancer – suggests we take it to his house, seeing as how he lives on the ground floor. By this time it is 3am, but we think, 'Fuck it, it's got to be done.'

We get to Martin's place and try to take the cake in. Slight mishap: it won't fit through his door. By this time, we're getting good at solving cake conundrums. No problem, we take out the window.

Mission accomplished. We clear the only two tables in the house and there it lies, in pride of place. Drive home. It's 4.30am.

9th October 1986, 9.30am.

The phone rings.

I pick it up and answer with an only slightly subdued 'Oy! Oy!'

'It's Louis…' the agent, 'You bastards! You've stolen Freddie Mercury's birthday cake!'

Me (quick as a flash): 'No we haven't. Er, it must have been some teenagers we saw when we were leaving.'

Louis: 'Well, the Management have called in the police. That cake cost £4,000.' Click.

I can admit to being slightly worried. A past indiscretion (theft of Cabinet Minister Peter Walker's Rolls-Royce, fraud, burglary, etc) meant that I spent much of the '70s in prison.

I ring Martin: 'Mart, they're on to us. I'm coming round.'

I go round.

Martin has a bright idea. 'We can't eat it, it's too big – let's give it to an old people's home. Old folks like cake.'

Brilliant. We phone the local old people's home which snaps up the offer of free cake for the foreseeable future.

Window frame out. Cake back in Transit.

As we drive away from Martin's house, I notice a police car coming from the opposite direction. They stop at Martin's, but luckily don't think to look in their rear-view mirror. If they had, they would have seen three feet of cake sticking out of the back of our van.

We deliver the cake to the Ranyard Memorial Nursing Home. Breathe a sign of relief and drive home.

9th October 1986, 4.30pm.
Asleep. The doorbell rings.
Answer door.
Two detectives from West End Central Police Station are standing on my doorstep.
Detective Number 1: 'You've stolen Freddie Mercury's birthday cake.'
Me: 'No, I haven't.'
Detective Number 2: 'Oh yes, you have.'
Me: 'This is a pantomime.'
Detective Number 1: 'Oh no, it's not.'
Me: 'Behind you!'
They barge in, produce a search warrant and – believe it or not – two magnifying glasses with which they search for cake crumbs. Needless to say they don't find any, and they leave, vowing to return.

That was almost ten years ago, and I've not heard a thing since.

Hang on, is that the door?

18
Ralph McTell
...remembers 'Laurel & Hardy'

S tan and Ollie first entered my life in 1951. My next door neighbour and friend, Charlie Ranger, had found himself with an extra sixpence in his pocket and had treated me to Saturday morning pictures at the Croydon Hippodrome – which for some reason was always known as the Odeon. I was an instant convert. In my absence my mum had reported me missing to the police, but I was so high after the adventure that my ration of 'coating' didn't deter me from thinking up ways and means of going back on a regular basis. I was six years old.

The 'Odeon' was a lovely old cinema with a balcony and boxes. It was sixpence downstairs, ninepence upstairs and on Saturday morning pictures it was packed with highly charged pre-teen kids. The noise was already cacophonous, but somehow got even louder as the lights were dimmed for The Chief's entrance. I suppose he was the manager and it was his job simultaneously to keep us under control and whip us up to a high pitch of feverish excitement. First of all, he told us to shut up, and then persuaded us to join in the communal singing of songs like *Jerusalem* (Blake) and *Alouette, Gentille Alouette*.

Next came the birthdays, and after the embarrassed and fortunate few (you got in free on your birthday) had returned to their seats after having *Happy Birthday* sung to them on stage, the place would darken. The noise level would explode again, and the show would begin.

After a cartoon, a comedy short, and a serial, came the main feature. Of all the films I saw, I remember the comedies best, and Laurel And Hardy best of all. I can't remember if I laughed out loud or even if I grinned in the dark, but Stan and Ollie touched me with their eternal optimism and genteel, impoverished charm. Sometimes I would get annoyed when Ollie acknowledged the presence of the camera, but only because I wanted to keep the magic intact and feel that I was the only one to see a way out of their predicaments. Although Ollie was looking at me from the screen, I couldn't help knowing that he was really looking at a camera.

It was at the Odeon that I first became aware of my own mortality. As kids, we assumed that all our favourites – Laurel And Hardy, The Bowery Boys, Abbott And Costello – were roughly contemporary, and when a newsreel announced that Laurel And Hardy were coming to tour the UK, it really shocked me to see them as lined-faced old men. The footage was all the more frightening – sinister, even – because they were wearing their little trademark bowler hats and smiling. Ollie, as usual, had his little finger held out, as if he were holding a porcelain tea-cup. It was a horror and an awakening I'd never forget.

In spite of being a big man, Ollie had tremendous grace. As slapstick comedians, Laurel And Hardy's incredible timing had more to do with dance than with knockabout comedy. It came as no surprise to discover that Ollie (or Babe, as all his real friends called him) was a marvellous ballroom dancer and among the first male Hollywood stars to be invited to showbiz parties. His services as a dancing partner were always in high demand, and even though he often tired as the night wore on, it is said that gallant Ollie never refused a lady's request. This gallantry was a part of his Southern upbringing: Babe was raised in Georgia by his mother and great aunt, whom he always addressed in the French manner as 'Tante'. When Babe flaps his tie in diversionary shyness, places the tips of his fingers together parson-like, or screws up his face in embarrassment when addressing the ladies, I see Tante's influence. Not only would he have absorbed all these mannerisms from his family, he would also have been aware of the values of true Southern hospitality and know the kind of behaviour expected of a Georgian gentleman. This graciousness came naturally to him, and because of the distressed circumstances of his screen roles, it added poignancy to his performance.

English-born Stan, on the other hand, was simply a genius. He was also an amazing craftsman who often spent hours working on a particular few moments in a scene. Stan had learned his stage craft in England and was already well-versed in the arts of pantomime and music hall long before he arrived in the States in the same troupe as Chaplin. Babe's film career was well established before he and Stan were teamed up by Hal Roach. They had appeared in the same two-reeler as early as 1918 (*The Lucky Dog*), but it took nine more years for *Should Married Men Go Home?* to be credited as the first Laurel And Hardy short. Ollie soon recognised Stan's superb comic talent and for the rest of their time together was content to let Stan make all the artistic decisions. 'Whatever Stan says is okay with me,' Ollie would reply when asked for a directorial or comedy decision.

I believe that the complete trust Hardy had in Stan's ability was the key to their success. There is not the slightest hint of rivalry or upstaging in their films, and – unlike many comic partnerships – they actually enjoyed each other's company away from the studio lot. Theirs was not a 'straight-man and funny-man' relationship, they were both funny men. The fat pompous one and the thin stupid one were both capable of making us laugh. Even as a kid I realised that their child-like understanding of the world really was child-like, and we loved them all the more for their innocence. Stan would offer up a ridiculous solution to a problem only to have Ollie (who had apparently seen its pitfalls), counter with an even sillier one.

Until Laurel And Hardy's teaming, American comedy was very broad, very slapstick and very fast. And although there is an undoubted slapstick element to the boys' work, their 'business' was positively graceful compared to what others were up to: it was ballet as distinct from the rest's Charleston. The pace of their comedy was also much slower (Stan took what must have seemed terrible risks to the studio bosses with his long silences) and even today, I am hard-pressed to think of anyone who dares leave such long gaps between lines.

Did Stan invent the comic close-up? I think of those marvellous moments as the camera scrutinises Stan's face as he ponders a problem. He almost arrives at a solution and opens his mouth to speak, only to stop and scratch his 'just got out of bed' sticking-up hair. While Stan's close-ups portray him lost in a world he doesn't fathom, Ollie's invite us in. We are offered the chance to share in his frustration at the numbskull he is required to take care of. The irony being, of course, that he is barely able to take care of himself.

I have often noted the contrast in their eyes. Just how did Stan achieve that totally dead-eyed look, when 'straight' photos show his eyes full of life and vitality? And in close-up, no one could fail to be moved by the softness and great humanity in Babe's eyes. What is so wonderful about these two is that in real life they were every bit as warm and kind as you would expect from their on-screen roles, as countless contemporaries have testified. I was particularly moved to read the accounts in John McCabe's biography, *Babe*, of supporting artists on a late English tour describing how big Ollie climbed several flights of stairs in order to collect their autographs as souvenirs. Yes, Laurel And Hardy as autograph hunters.

We saw dozens of Laurel And Hardy shorts at the flicks – silents as well as talkies – and occasionally full length features. These ranged from the brilliant *Way Out West* to their last, and truly dreadful, *Robinson Crusoe Land* (AKA *Atoll K*), which was filmed in three languages with as many directors. Although many of their best films are credited to Hal Roach, Stan actually did most of the directing. Professional jealousy might explain why Roach found it necessary to tamper with so many of their films after the event. Two of the most irrational interferences appear in *Swiss Miss*, with the insertion of the gorilla in the end scene, and the ruining of the piano gag. Roach removed the scene where we see the piano key of 'middle C' being connected to a bomb, and so makes the ensuing close-ups of the boys' hands almost hitting it completely pointless. Luckily, this didn't stop the movie from being a great success: it would have taken more than a spot of shoddy editing to do that.

My favourite Laurel And Hardy movie – after much soul-searching – is probably *Way Out West*. It could have been a success with any pair of competent comic actors in the lead roles, but with the boys, it is superb. The plot of *Way Out West* is pure melodrama: the rightful heiress is deprived of her inheritance by her villainous boss and his floozy. The twist is that well-intentioned Ollie and Stan are the cause of her problem, even if they do eventually come to her rescue and – by default – save the day. From the moment we see our heroes' carefree gait as they walk over the hill with their mule, all our cares begin to vanish. A favourite scene is the one where the floozy tries to tickle the map out of Stan's grasp in her boudoir. It appeared as if the director had to abandon any hope of a 'clean take', the actress is laughing hysterically, and so, apparently, is Stan. For a Laurel And Hardy film, I think this scene is incredibly sexy.

Stan and Ollie are often caught in bed together, but there is no thought of any naughtiness. Our only concerns are to do with who has the lion's share of the blankets, who has to get up to turn out the light, and which of them is going to investigate the mysterious noise. When Stan and Ollie appear with wives in films, their partners are usually harridans of the first order. We wonder why on earth they married the boys in the first place, and as far as sex is concerned, the very idea that the marriage might ever have been consummated is too ridiculous to contemplate. The wives are there either as additional authority figures or else (and more dangerously) to draw the boys away from us and in to the real, adult world of complex sexual politics and proper responsibilities. But, thank goodness, they are never allowed to succeed.

It's strange to see what still makes us laugh from the old films. Stan and Ollie's gentle art was replaced by the likes of Abbott and Costello, The Three Stooges and Martin And Lewis, and double acts continue to be big box office. But these later comics had a different and more predictable format: straight man/funny man, handsome/plain, clever/stupid. I enjoyed them all in their different ways, but looking back, they've all dated badly. Chaplin is a link to the humour of the Victorians, Abbott and Costello represent the fast-talking '40s, Martin and Lewis the '50s and early '60s, but Stan and Ollie are timeless.

Children love them because they are at least as smart as they are, and as we grow older, their innocence and child-like optimism has the power to lift our jaded spirits. Those of us who are even remotely connected with the entertainment business can only marvel at their skill, humanity, and timing. Their catchphrases are still with us, and let's face it, when it comes to character-led comedy, Laurel And Hardy wrote the book.

Whenever I am appearing at a theatre I know they performed in, I get an added buzz. Towards the end of their career, they toured Britain quite extensively; I often wonder if I might be sharing their dressing room, and try and guess as to what they would have said to each other. Somehow I can't believe that they would ever have run out of things to discuss. Some bands I know only get through the grind and repetition of life on the road by playing cards and trying to win money from each other, but that doesn't sound like Laurel And Hardy to me. I can tell that they were pals to the end.

Their last scene together was in 1957 and was held in private. I can only guess at the script. Babe had suffered a series of strokes that had left him paralysed and unable to speak. But somehow he was able to indicate that he wanted to see his old friend and partner one last time. Stan never talked about that last scene but we know that he was greatly distressed by it. In my mind I can see Ollie's eyes looking imploringly up at Stan from the bed.

Another fine mess?

I see Stan turning his hands palms upwards and raising his eyebrows and looking nowhere in particular for inspiration. Perhaps he scratches his head, starts as if to speak, and then pauses to think again. He repeats these familiar gestures as if in a film. Ollie indicates a smile, Stan's bottom lip begins to quiver, his eyes screw up and real tears begin to fall. He looks at his friend and partner once more. Ollie indicates a smile but real tears fall too. Stan makes one last attempt to speak, but nothing comes out. With eyebrows raised, he lifts his hand to his face and, moving his fingers in a downward flick beginning with the little finger, he mouths the word 'bye'. He walks to the door and leaves the room. It ends, as it began in the silents, in silence.

Cue: *The March Of The Cuckoos…*

19
John Hegley

...'The stand up comedian sits down'

the comedian climbs onto the stage

and truthfully points out

that the microphone smells of sick

so does your breath says somebody

get on with it says somebody else

please settle down

replies the comedian responding well

I'll start this routine if it kills me

there is an outbreak of cheering

at the mention of his death

get off says the one who said get on with it

and the comedian comes up with a line

so apt and incisive

that any further heckling is redundant

unfortunately he comes up with it

on the bus home

20
Anita Chaudhuri
...examines the role of 'Women in Comedy'

I once interviewed a female clown, Danise Payne, who trained with the fabled Ringling Brothers circus troupe in Florida. 'Women make good clowns,' she claimed, 'Because you have to have a good sense of humour to be a woman in this life. And hell, if we ever get stuck for new material, we can always bring our personal lives into comedy.'

She has a point. Women are handed a lifetime's worth of great potential script material almost from the moment they are born. If only we could all remember to jot down all those lousy chat-up lines, lame excuses and tall stories that inevitably come our way, there would be many more women storming the citadel of the BBC Light Entertainment Department.

The fact that so many female comedians focus on the weaknesses of men and the pitfalls of being a woman, could account in part for why there are still relatively few comedy megababes breaking through to the mainstream. Other women may find them hilariously funny, but a roster of largely male TV executives, agents and A & R men don't necessarily want them around. Women have been making fun of men for a lot longer than they've been allowed air-time for their jokes. In the twenties and thirties, women took up the pen rather than the mike-stand to get their jokes across. Edna Ferber, a now largely forgotten wit and member of Dorothy Parker's Round Table earned a comfortable living by penning lines such as: 'Being an old maid is like death by drowning, a really delightful sensation after you cease to struggle.' Then there was Anita Loos, whose whole *Gentlemen Prefer Blondes* saga was nothing but a celebration of the gullibility of the male sex.

By the 1930s and 1940s, however, the best vehicle for female wit had become the movies, in particular the sudden rash of screwball comedies that dominated the period. There were plenty of contenders, but no actress could beat Mae West at the male-trashing one-liner, both on and off-screen. 'I was once so poor I didn't know where my next husband was coming from,' she once told an interviewer.

The Golden Age soon passed though, and now we are faced with an entertainment industry which is irritatingly reluctant to accept women who are both sexy and funny. Bland blonde bombshells like Goldie Hawn and Meg Ryan just about get away with it, but even when Ryan was enacting her infamous restaurant orgasm scene in *When Harry Met Sally*, she seemed strangely sexless, too sugary to represent sexual threat.

The only real way for women to become comedy megababes today is the hard way, through good old-fashioned, nerve-wracking stand-up routines. Since the '80s and the advent of French and Saunders, Ruby Wax and Victoria Wood, women have for the first time had viable comedy role models. Whether or not they are good role models is another matter entirely. Personally, I think it would be better if there were more women out there who were a bit more ordinary and a bit more willing to cater for female audiences.

Whoever first said 'comedy is the new rock n roll' got it completely wrong, at least as far as women are concerned. Comedy, unlike the music industry, doesn't welcome babes who a) look like supermodels, b) sleep with the lead guitarist, or, c) hang groupie-like around stage doors. On the contrary, it often seems to be *de rigueur* for successful comediennes to have the build of a sumo wrestler, the wardrobe of a confirmed catalogue shopper and the voice of a regional British Rail platform announcer. Women who don't conform to this image tend to languish, forgotten about, in the hinterland of trendy North London clubs. Look at Hattie Hayridge, blonde, talented and the sexiest woman in British comedy since Hattie Jacques. A prime-time TV show? No, no dearie, you just stick to being a hologram for the time being... And there are plenty more comedy wallflowers like her. Ronnie Ancona and Rhona Cameron to name but two. Jenny Eclair's still waiting for the big one and Donna McPhail, surely a worthy replacement for Jasper Carrott, has only snuck into the mainstream via her role as presenter of *The Sunday Show*.

Of any comedian in Britain today, Victoria Wood is the most successful, having packed out the Royal Albert Hall for more nights than Eric Clapton and holding her own in the Morecambe and Wise Christmas TV slot. Her cosy comedy is dull and not particularly gender specific, which is of course why she's so massively popular. But she has paved the way for more outrageous artists such as Jo Brand to enter the mainstream.

When Wood was starting out there were no female role models in the industry and she had to make do with hero-worshipping Joyce Grenfell, who she went to see at the age of six. For Wood there was no tradition of 'alternative comedy' and no clubs beyond the rabid working men's circuit. 'Women weren't allowed into those clubs unless they were really, really glamorous or really, really sort of aggressively ugly and bizarre. There was no place for just looking ordinary. I had to wait for it to change,' she has said.

Those were the days when the subject matter chosen by comedians was a million galaxies away from those subjects guaranteed to make women laugh. In time-honoured Les

Dawson tradition, women were usually the butt of all jokes, or were ignored altogether. Of all the '90s comediennes, it is Jo Brand who has turned tradition on its head with a vengeance. This, after all, is the woman whose catchphrase is 'Never trust a man with testicles'. Unlike Dawn French, Brand is fat and proud of it, characteristically getting the insults in first before anyone else seizes the chance. 'Doctor, I think I've got a stomach problem,' 'You have, it's bloody enormous' boom-boom. Not for her the tastefully-posed nude shots in *Esquire* magazine or the trendy clothing emporia for larger women so favoured by French. If you are a man and you dare to express revulsion at her unkempt image, then, in her words, you can get 'bobbitted'. Small wonder that many of her detractors assume, incorrectly, that she is a lesbian.

Brand's comedy focuses on food and beauty and her repertoire contains a litany of peculiarly female subjects, heretofore unchartered in comedy – cream cakes, male inadequacies, PMT, thrush, clitorises, penises and diets. There has never been anyone quite like Brand before on the British comedy scene, but in America she does have a counterpart, and no, it isn't Roseanne. Had Brand been born in the Hollywood Hills, she'd have metamorphosed into Sandra Bernhard, another man-chewing comedienne whose central themes are feminism and beauty. Bernhard is simply a slimmed down Brand with a Las Vegas makeover – just add some singing lessons and a handful of famous friends and *hey presto!*

Like Brand, Bernhard survived the stand-up circuit by building up a reputation for being able to out-heckle the hecklers. 'What are you wearing?' she once snarled at a lesbian couple in her audience. 'Have you both just come from a hooker convention?' She's also quick to get in first with the insults. 'I have one of those hard-to-believe faces,' she breathes in the opening credits of her film 'Without You I'm Nothing'. She's not kidding: her features arrange themselves in an approximation of a wide-mouthed frog who's had a crash with the Clinique counter. She looks hysterical before she ever opens her mouth to tell a joke, and when she eventually does, her voice is a comedy in its own right, sounding as it does like a cross between Jackie Mason and Jessica Rabbit.

Bernhard is a fine illustration of the difference between British and American comediennes. She embraces the good-old fashioned all-singing, all-dancing variety tradition, with plenty of Burt Bacharach cover versions (even if they are hilarious send-ups) and Vegas-style costume changes. Who can forget her rendition of *Stop in the Name of Love*, where, clad in a turquoise sequinned evening gown and Diana Ross wig, she sings 'Stop! Do you have any rubbers? And while you're at it, what about some spermicidal creams and jellies...' In America, comedy is allowed to collide with glamour.

This is also plainly evident in the American TV industry. There has long been a tradition of snappy, sassy female-led sitcoms, from *Rhoda* and *Mary Tyler Moore* in the '70s to Kate and *Allie*, *Ellen*, *Grace Under Fire and Roseanne* in recent years. Most of these feature dizzy, ditzy heroines grappling with runaway domestic appliances and runaway dates from hell and are deplorably well-telegraphed in their scripting. But hell, they get to live in adorable apartments, and with the exception of *Ellen*, get to wear the grooviest clothes on television.

Meanwhile we have to make do with the seemingly indestructible *Birds of a Feather*, a sitcom which features three of the most brain-dead specimens of womankind ever allowed out on day-release. It's true that *Absolutely Fabulous* helped to temporarily alter the state of things, but there are to be no more series of this gem. It's no coincidence that this is the first comedy to have established a massive fan following in America since the days of Benny Hill and *Monty Python*.

It's not that American sitcoms are perfect, but they do often give women the chance to be genuinely funny. Sometimes

TV executives get a bit antsy about the dominance of funny, sexy women ruling the roost, and decide to spoil the party. This happened with *Kate and Allie;* when producers decided the duo were getting too big for their boots they retaliated by marrying Allie off to a singularly colourless individual whom she'd know for about four days. Things haven't changed much, except that the wardrobes are getting grungier viz *Roseanne* and *Ellen*. Ellen DeGeneres, for it is she who plays Ellen Morgan of the same series, cut her teeth on the stand-up circuit before she seized her own show. Critics have hailed her as 'the funniest person in America' which is no mean feat given the competition that nation offers – including the mighty Dan Quayle. Of course Ellen really is the funniest person in America, but not because of her endless antics with customers in her bookstore or with retarded boyfriends, but because of her wardrobe. She must surely be the only comedienne in America who is forced to wear cast offs from the remnants of the *Dick Van Dyke Show* wardrobe department.

The reason for the success of *Ellen*, rather like that of *AbFab* is that it's comedy at its most aspirational: most women want to be Ellen, or Edina or Patsy. And therein lies an essential truth about successful female comedians. We laugh at them because we find them funny. Let's just leave it at that.

21
Norman Lovett
...gets worked up about 'Litter'

I was reading an article recently in which a 14-year old girl asked: 'What chance has the world of survival, when so many people still litter?'

And I have to say, it's a thought that's gone through my mind many times. Do you litter? There's no grey area in this matter. You either litter or you don't. I don't. In fact quite a lot of us don't.

I know we've all seen people who screw up their fish and chip wrapping into a very tight, neat ball and pop it gently on to the kerb. But I'm sorry: they are still litterers. These are the cowardly and shy litterers, unable to emit the energy of a full-blown litterer. The blatant litterer who just drops it where he or she happens to be.

I once watched a very fat boy coming out of Woolworth's loaded down with confectionery. He stood on the corner and consumed the lot in under five minutes. As he attempted to walk off, he collapsed in to a knee-high pile of his own confectionery wrappings. He was so fat he could hardly get up, and when he eventually did, he went straight back into Woolworth's for a second helping.

You can't always spot a litterer. They don't all wear red and have the same star sign. I was walking behind a lager-lout recently who was eating fish and chips. He had six earrings in each ear, heavily tattooed arms and forehead, steel toe-capped boots and wore a capped-sleeve T-shirt in the sub-zero temperature. A born litterer if you ever saw one, you'd think. But no, when he had popped the last six squashed-up chips into his cement mixer of a mouth, he screwed up the wrapping paper, threw it into the air and head-butted it into the nearest litter bin. I was so impressed I started clapping.

Unfortunately he then set fire to the contents of the litter bin and threatened to knock my head off for looking at him. But at least he wasn't a litterer.

The ultimate litterer is the one who drops it where he or she stands. None of this screwing up, they just let it float to the ground without even looking at it. The ultimate litterer has an IQ of 3. The ultimate litterer will not be reading this, but perhaps someone will read it to him. If I can stop one person littering, then my work in this world will have been worthwhile.

The reason I have become obsessive about litter is because of where I live. My house is exactly halfway along a very short, narrow one-way street. The roads at each end are very busy, one being a High Street. When it's windy, strong gusts blast along from both ends and meet outside my house. They greet each other before exchanging gifts of litter. The piles of litter outside my door can be enormous. Once a pile was so high, it became snow-capped.

The one thing I am grateful for is that the wind can't blow dog poo along. Imagine getting one blown into your face? That would almost be as bad as being kissed by Barbara Cartland.

There's someone near where I live who picks up their dog's poo, puts it in a small plastic bag and then dumps it on the kerb. So, basically this person is dropping litter with a soft centre – depending on the temperature of course. Actually I don't mind dog poo in the summer because the heat soon dries them out and makes them go crusty, and they disperse easily into the air. And you thought it was pollen that was giving you hay fever?

Anyway, that's enough about dog poo, because – although a form of litter – it is a subject I could write a book about. (Albeit a small book.)

I have been compiling a league table of litter over the last couple of years and crisp packets are the Manchester United of litter. When people are coming to see me, I don't have to tell them my address, I just ask them to follow any empty crisp packet that might happen along. Where it stops is where I live. In fact I wish crisp packets were much bigger because then I could ask people to get in and have a lift to my house.

I've been thinking of starting a 'spot the litter' competition but it's actually impossible to take a photograph with only one piece of litter in the frame. The fastest piece of litter was a Coca-Cola can that got caught in a gale and rolled along a motorway at 96mph. A police car gave chase and eventually forced it into a lay-by where it was given a breathyliser test which proved positive. It had been drinking rum all day.

The only answer to the litter problem is to get rid of packaging. Sell crisps loose, by the small shovel-full. Straight into the mouth or pocket. Coke could be served from a petrol pump affair, out of the nozzle straight into the cake-hole. The money saved on packaging would mean the product would be cheaper. The storage jar industry would quadruple overnight. What about radio-controlled packaging that on removal would make its way to the nearest recycling centre?

I suppose I'm getting silly now, but it was probably daft of me to think we could stop littering in the first place. And think how many road-sweepers would be out of work if litter didn't exist? What would they do? Get paper rounds but not deliver the newspapers; just screw them up and chuck them in to the road so they could get their original jobs back.

'This calls for a celebration, gentlemen. Let's open a can of worms.'

22
Dwight Z Giannetti

...'The Craft of Being Funny: Comedy and its Role in Western Culture During the Latter Part of the Twentieth Century.'

As innovative English humorist Max Boyce so wryly observed: 'comedy is a very serious business'. And surely Professor Rainier can not have been the first to recognise that this is a subject 'far too serious to be left to the comedians'?

Comedy is, without doubt, the most nebulous of all the arts. I have come across many attempts at pinning down its essence – ranging from: 'putting your foot in a bucket of water' (Norman Wisdom) to 'I can't remember that much about it, but I used to wear working denims and carry a banjo... I think' (Stringbean Akeman) – but when it comes right down to it, comedy is, by its very nature, totally indefinable. Whoever coined the expression 'light entertainment' was way off -mark. As my many successful students will testify, I prefer the term 'heavy entertainment'. And with total justification.

As Associate Professor of Comedy and

Neuropsychology at the University of West Carolina, I am often asked 'what is funny'. The answer I usually give is far too complex to go into here. It would take several thousand words and an increase in fee of at least a thousand dollars to do the subject any kind of justice. But, as luck would have it, the solution to that particular conundrum takes up the first three quarters of my most recent book, *Keep It Snappy: Timing and the Conceptionalisation Of Comedy and Comedians Within The Framework Of 20th Century American Popular Culture* (New York: Gusset & Dunlop, 1993; $8.99), available at most good bookshops or by mail-order from the address contained at the end of this chapter.

If we cannot explore the question 'what is funny', at least we can tackle the lesser issue of 'how do we write comedy and make a living out of it without having to be particularly gifted in the first place?'. At my world-famous Giannetti Comedy Seminars® I answer that very question. It may take two days and lots and lots of hard work (plus a very reasonable $899 + taxes) before I can turn turn a no-hoper with a beard and a stress problem in to a successful comedy writer with a beard and an acute stress problem, but you can easily recoup that paltry amount just by writing one article on *The Craft Of Being Funny: Comedy and its Role in Western Culture During the Latter Part of the Twentieth Century.*

Another question people often ask me is: 'why do people keep asking you all these questions?' That is because I am a comedy guru. It kind of comes with the territory. More to the point is the question: 'can comedy can be taught as a subject?' The answer is simple. Do bears eat porridge? Did Rubens go for fat broads? (The answer is 'yes' to both those rhetorical questions, by the way.) Of course you can teach people how to be funny. Do you think David Letterman learned it by himself?

What follows is a short extract from Day One (The Wanting Day©) of my Giannetti Comedy Seminar® on

Comedy Writing, in which I reveal many of the secrets of the craft. To find out more, simply enrol for the full course and send a cheque or postal order for only $899 (+ taxes) to the address at the end of this chapter. There is even a foolproof guarantee. If you do not recoup all this money – and more! – within two months of successfully completing my course, I will personally guarantee to commiserate with you on your exceeding bad fortune by means of personalised, hand-signed, photocopied letter.

The First Rule of Comedy is not to trust any of the hundreds of First Rules of Comedy that will be offered to you during your apprenticeship. Most of these consist of just one apposite word or phrase: for example, 't-t-t-timing', 'conflict' and 'no puns'. One contact at the British Broadcasting Corporation assures me that the real First Rule of Comedy is 'go to Balliol', but this only seems to apply within the United Kingdom. No, the First Rule of Comedy is that there is no First Rule of Comedy.

Similarly there are just as many Three Rules Of Comedy, all of which work on a single comic premise: ie, to repeat the First Rule of Comedy three times. For example: 'no puns, no puns, no puns'; 'conflict, conflict, conflict'; and 'there is no First Rule of Comedy, there is no First Rule of Comedy, there is no First Rule of Comedy'. Some work better than others. The First Rule of Comedy is that there are no genuine Three Rules of Comedy. If there were any genuine Three Rules of Comedy, they would be: 'there are no genuine Three Rules of Comedy, there are no genuine Three Rules of Comedy, there are no genuine Three Rules of Comedy.'

But the so-called Three Rules Of Comedy *(the ones that don't exist, remember?)* do serve three very useful purposes. (1) They show us that repetition can be funny, (2) they demonstrate the valuable 'Rule of Three', and (3) a zebra. The 'Rule of Three' shows that when building to a punchline, two builds is too few and four too many. The third item should always be the funny one. As in: '(1) They show us that repetition can be funny, (2) they demonstrate the 'Rule of Three', and (3) a zebra'.

Repetition can be very funny. In my book, *Gee, That's Really Funny, Mom: Language and the Development Of Comedy Within The Brain-Damaged Community Of Geezer County and Environs* (Los Angeles: Friedman & Caesar, 1981) – now only available thru mail-order, $8.99 + taxes, address at the end of this chapter – I point out that repetition has long been the staple diet of network situation comedies. From *Mr Ed* (CBS, 1961-65) thru *My Mother The Car* (NBC 1965-66) to *Get Smart* (NBC 1965-69; CBS '60-70), and coming right up to date with *Soap* (ABC 1977-) and *Cheers* (NBC, 1982-), the repetition of catch-phrases and even storylines as a means of humor is widespread. The 'running gag' is another example of how repetition helped make comedy king. The knocking over of the vase that invariably occurs near the start of every episode of *My Mother, The Tube of Superglue* (CBS 1981-1981) is a comic invention to rival Chaplin's eating of the bootlaces and Jack Benny's most polished violin routines. The Mother's inevitable use of the catch-phrase, 'having a smashing time, Darren?' and his 'get stuck in, Mum' retort, are guaranteed to bring the house down every time. (Knowledgeable readers will not be surprised to learn that I was a writer on *My Mother, The Tube of Superglue* for its entire run. That is, up until those narrow-minded, money-men at the network cancelled it in favour of the dire *My Uncle, The Talking Spider Plant* [CBS 1981-88].)

But, to return to our 'rule of three', there is no logical reason why the gratuitous use of the word 'zebra' (above) should make us laugh. But it does. Any burlesque veteran will tell you that some words are funny and others are not. No one quite knows why the funny ones are funny, they just are. Go up to any man in any bar anywhere in the American-speaking world and say 'balloon'. Watch his reaction. If, on the other hand, the word were to be 'motherfucker', the result would be a totally different. Try it for yourself, I think you'll find it an interesting experiment.

The next best thing to enrolling in a Giannetti Comedy Seminar® is to read the right books. If you value your sanity and any sense of comic timing you may already have developed, avoid Dr Freud's *Der Witz und seine Beziehung zum Unbewussten (Jokes and How they Relate to the Subconcious)* at all costs. It sucks. *Der Witz und seine Beziehung zum Unbewussten (Jokes and How they Relate to the Subconcious)* is a perfect example of how not to write about comedy. But you can't blame Freud. If only he'd been able to attend a Giannetti Comedy Seminar® – in which I reveal many of the hidden secrets of the trade – he'd have been much less obsessed with people wanting to have sex with their maternal parents and more interested in the business of making people laugh.

Two further books – in addition to the titles already mentioned – I can heartily recommend to every aspiring student of comedy are *Who's That Zany Man?: The Craft of Cousin Jody and his Innovative Role in the Comedy Movement of Southern and Central Tennessee 1927-46* by Dwight Z Giannetti (Nashville: Travis & Tritt, 1991; $8.99), and *Watch Your Dirty Mouth, a Study Of Sex and Sexuality in Comedy and its Relationship to the Female Stand-Up Comics of the Alaskan Alternative Comedy Circuit* (Juneau AK: UNEAP, University Of North-Eastern Alaska Press, 1992; $8.99). Both rip away the dead skin, get right to the heart of comedy, and tear it out, holding it aloft and shouting: 'eureka! eureka! And you bastards said I'd never work in comedy again!'

I'll close with a short extract from *Keep It Snappy: Timing and the Conceptionalisation Of Comedy and Comedians Within The Framework Of 20th Century American Popular Culture* (New York: Gusset & Dunlop, 1993; $8.99), which is pretty autobiographical: 'My first writing role in a networked sitcom was as trainee writer (number fourteen) in the highly original *My Favourite Uncle From Mars* (NBC 1967-67). The simple but brilliant premise was that a one-seater flying saucer from Mars crash-lands near San Francisco, the occupant (Jerry Delgardo) is res-cued by a young newspaper reporter called Tom O'Hare (Danny Heidelman), who passes him off as his "Uncle Malcolm". Malcolm helps Tom get newspaper stories and gen-erally uses his extra-terrestrial powers to help out, often with unexpected and hilarious consequences.

'During the short run of the show, I made my way up from Trainee Writer (number fourteen) to Trainee Writer (num-ber six), largely thanks to a brilliant exchange I wrote between Tom and Malcolm in episode three, "Is There No Cure For The Martian Cold?" In this episode, Malcolm cannot stop himself from sneezing, and being a Martian, every time he sneezes, he disappears.

'TOM: *Why do you keep doing that?*

'MALCOLM: *Doing what? Atchoo!*

'TOM: *Disappearing! You keep disappearing!*

'MALCOLM: *Atchoo! It's one of the side-effects of the Martian Cold. I can't help it. Atchoo!*

'TOM: *You're worse than Mrs Doretsky down at the bakery.*

'MALCOLM: *Atchoo! Why, does she keep disappearing?*

'TOM: *No, but she never stops sneezing. She's allergic to wheatflour.*

'MALCOLM: *Atchoo! Then why on earth does she work at the bakery?*

'TOM: *You've got to make your bread somehow!* (beat) *But come to think of it, she did disappear a couple of times last year – but it was with that bran salesman from Albuquerque!'*

'Notice how the 'topper' gag about the salesman fol-lows the line about making 'your bread somehow!'. The Topper is an important tool in comedy, but it should always be used sparingly and wisely. You will really need to attend a Seminar to learn the essentials about that. And I know just the one...'

(The rest of this chapter has been omitted by the Editor in the interests of good taste).
Professor Giannetti can be contacted at The University Of West Carolina, c/o Dwight's $1 Bargain Basement, 55672B One-Hundred-And-Ninety-Ninth Street, Millersberg, West Carolina, 99911999, USA.*

23
Comedy Great:
...Will Hay's 'First Day at School' (1938)

The following extract is taken from Will Hay's famous 'Schoolmaster Comedian' stage routine. Hay toured the theatres and music halls of Britain with this act until his retirement from the stage in 1939. A version of the down-at-heel schoolmaster made his first appearance in 1909, and the routine passed through many changes and refinements before evolving in to the polished, finely-crafted 20-minute sketch we see represented here.

The Schoolmaster character, slightly less than resplendent in mortar-board, gown, pince-nez, and sporting a dangerously swishy cane, featured in several of Hay's feature films – most notably, *Boys Will Be Boys* (1935) and *Good Morning, Boys* (1937) – before making his final public appearance in a BBC radio series, *Diary of a Schoolmaster*, broadcast from 1942 until a debilitating stroke ended Hay's performing career in 1946.

Today Hay is remembered for his classic Gainsborough film comedies, the best of which are *Oh, Mr Porter!* (1937) and *Ask A Policeman* (1939). But he never appeared on stage with his regular screen companions, Moore Marriott ('the old fool') and Graham Moffatt ('the boy'). The pair did get to perform these routines on stage, but only with Hay's son, Will Hay Jr, who tried to revive his father's act in variety theatres after the War.

During the War, Hay – who was over forty at its out-break – served as a lieutenant-instructor in the Sea Cadet Corps. Although he left school without any formal qualifications, he managed to teach himself German, Italian and French. Hay was a keen amateur astronomer, and in 1935 wrote a book called *Through My Telescope: Astronomy For All* which became an recognised textbook on the subject. He was made a Fellow of the Royal Astronomical Society after discovering a white spot on Saturn.

It is the first day of term at Hay's new school and two pupils arrive: a boy and an old man. Part of the humour stems from the fact that the boy is cleverer than Hay, and that both of them are smarter than the old man. The old man is also partially deaf, which doesn't help in sorting out his details. Hay manages to ascertain that the old man has lost his job as a wheel-tapper on the railways, and this is why (using typically woolly music hall logic) he comes to be returning to school at such an advanced age.

Admirers of Abbott and Costello's brilliant 'Who's On Next' routine – which this sketch pre-dates – should appreciate the humour.

Hay starts to take the register…

HAY *(to boy)*: I'll have your name first.

BOY: Wye.

HAY: Why? There's no particular reason why, simply that you came in first. You see, it doesn't matter to me whether I have your name first or his, only I'm expecting a bit of bother with him, so I thought I'd settle yours. Well, come on, what is it?

BOY: Wye.

HAY:	Well, when you open a school one of the first things that you do, after the school is built and the mortgage arranged, is to buy a register, and in it you enter the names of the boys.
BOY:	Yes.
HAY:	Well, I've bought this, and I'm going to use it. Well come on, what is it?
BOY:	Wye.
HAY:	Because I want to put it in the book.
BOY:	Well, put it in the book.
HAY:	I will, when I know it.
BOY:	But you do know it!
HAY:	No I don't!
BOY:	Well you ought to.
HAY:	Why?
BOY:	Yes.
HAY *(to Old Man)*:	Have you got your hammer with you?
BOY:	Don't you understand - my name is Wye.
HAY:	Oh, your name is Wye - I thought you were being inquisitive. *(To Old Man)* His name's Wye.
OLD MAN:	Why?
HAY:	To see if they're sound.

After this, Hay finds out that the boy's names are Arthur Court, which he mishears as "Alf a quart'. After a struggle, Hay finally gets the boy's names right. But it's not all perfect sailing...

HAY:	Arthur Court Wye.
BOY:	Because those are my names.
HAY:	That's what I've got, Arthur Court Wye.

BOY:	Because I was christened that.
HAY:	I know you were. Shut up, I know what I'm doing. Arthur – Court – W-Y-E. Where do you live?
BOY:	Streatham.
HAY:	That's SE.
BOY:	16.
HAY:	I know, I know a girl… there's a girls' school round there somewhere. *(To Old Man)* And what do they call you?
OLD MAN:	Eh?
HAY:	What do they call you?
OLD MAN:	Barmy.
HAY:	Yes, and you look it, but I can't put 'barmy' in the book. I want your proper name.
OLD MAN:	Oh, me proper name.
HAY:	Yes.
OLD MAN:	Reginald Clarence D'Arcy.
HAY:	Joe what?
OLD MAN:	No, Reginald Clarence D'Arcy.
HAY:	Reginald Clarence D'Arcy. And you worked on the railway with a name like that.
OLD MAN:	Yes.
HAY:	D'Arcy - that's an old French name.
OLD MAN:	Yes.
HAY:	Came over with the Conqueror?
OLD MAN:	Yes.
HAY:	Were you seasick?
OLD MAN:	No.
HAY:	Well, where do you live?
OLD MAN:	Eh?
HAY:	I said, where do you live?

OLD MAN: Ware.

HAY: Yes.

OLD MAN: Yes.

HAY: No, I said, where do you live?

OLD MAN: Ware.

HAY: Yes.

OLD MAN: Yes.

HAY: He's as deaf as a post. I said, where do you live?

OLD MAN: Ware.

HAY: Yes.

OLD MAN: Yes.

HAY (*To Boy*): You see what tapping wheels does.

OLD MAN (*getting annoyed*): Don't you know Ware?

HAY: If I knew where, I wouldn't ask, would I?

The one on the right's an alternative comedian...'

24
Mark Steel
...on 'Fame'

The tortured soul of the successful comedian has been
analysed through the centuries – tragic tears behind the
face of the clown, the internal agonies of Hancock or
Lenny Bruce. On the other hand, the failed comedian is the
subject of many a study: as in *The King of Comedy* and *The
Entertainer*. But have you ever considered the indignity, suffering and torment, the lack of any identity in society of the
Slightly Successful Comedian?

No longer trucking round the clubs on a bill with
Jimmy Riddle ('Funny' – *The Bedford Anarchist*) or Archie
Astonishing And His Juggling Licorice Allsorts, but not well
known enough to attract more than 70 fans to the smaller of the
two rooms in the smaller of the two theatres in the average
town, as he arrives passing a bustling queue for *Murder At The
Tennis Club*, starring a bloke who was in one series of *London's
Burning*, in the 400-seat auditorium upstairs.

The struggling comedian can look forward to an
appearance on TV that will change his life forever. The Slightly
Successful Comedian has been on TV and the next morning
had to do his own laundry.

The marvellous thing about struggling is you know
where you stand. Once in Norwich I went on stage at a minia-
ture rock festival in front of 300 students who were screaming
for a band called Fuzzbox who had been due on an hour before,

but who were running behind schedule. Forty seconds later the promoter was delicately wiping a pulsating globule of gob from my shirt and ordering a roadie to sweep a glistening path of smashed Thunderbird wine and cider bottles from the stage. Later, as I tried to get to sleep sharing a settee with a Saint Bernard in the promoter's squat, I proudly felt part of a living tradition, that of 'the struggling comedian on the road'.

Compare that to the mind-twisting experience some years later of getting two encores after a 90-minute show to 200 people in Leicester, then ten minutes later waiting outside for a bus to the bed and breakfast while two blokes growled: 'You'd better not be pushing in mate,' while their girlfriends protested, 'Oh leave 'im Kev, 'e's all on 'is own.'

Or what about the emotional turmoil of the night I appeared on a programme called *Sunday, Sunday* with Gloria Hunniford? The other guests were Barry McGuigan, Jan Francis and John Alderton. For an hour or so after the show we chatted, drank and joked together: professional entertainers relaxing after the hard slog, of talking for eight minutes each in front of a camera. 'Good luck with the new telly series,' I said to Jan as we parted. 'And good luck with that gig you're doing in a pub in Bradford,' she replied. Less than an hour later I was dragging a mattress into the living room of my Tulse Hill council flat because water was dripping through the ceiling in the bedroom. How are you supposed to cope with enforced schizophrenia like that?

There are two crushing insults you can make to the Slightly Successful Comedian. The first is to go up straight after a storming show and say, 'That was really good mate. So do you actually make a living out of this then?' This is the equivalent of getting a plumber round and as he's reaching behind the washing machine, asking, 'So what do you do as a day job then?' The correct response to this question is to tell them you earn between £20,000 and £30,000 a week.

The other insult is to say, 'Oh you're a comedian are you? Well who knows, one day you might be famous'. This approach supposes that: (a) you clearly crave fame, and (b) you even more clearly haven't got it because I've never heard of you, mate. Therefore you are, so far at least, a failure.

To this you must reply that fame is the most appalling possible yardstick to measure success by. David Mellor, after all, is famous. So is Keith Chegwin. And Myra Hindley and Jeremy Beadle and Alan Titchmarsh and Reggie Kray and that irritating twat who introduces *Countdown*.

Bamber Gascoigne is famous. I know because I once saw him arrive at a theatre, and as he was collecting his tickets a security guard shouted at him: 'Oy mate, here's your starter for ten. Hoah haah.' Whether it annoys him or not that every time he goes to a shop he has to expect the assistant to say something like: 'And what would you like? No conferring, I'll have to hurry you…' I don't know. But it surely can't have been his life's ambition.

At the time of writing there is regularly on television an advert for toothpaste with three actors playing dancing teeth singing something along the lines of: 'We're all smiling because now we get smothered twice a day in new oxygenated Crest. Mmmm.' At one and the same time those actors have attained the height of their fame and the peak of their failure.

So it is that I can reassure myself that semi-obscurity is healthy. That a project such as my current one of writing a radio play that will go out at 10.45pm on Radio 4 to 20,000 retired antiques dealers dotted around the Home Counties is far more worthwhile than going on a BBC1 TV panel show and scoring two extra points for singing the theme to *The Wombles* with Robin Asquith.

So slightly successful comedians know full well the limitations of fame as a gauge of value to society. But they also know that if they look out of the window and see the postman they think: 'Ah, there's the postman,' whereas if they looked out of the window and saw Des Lynam they'd shout: 'Fuck me, there's that bloke off the telly.'

Which is why it does feel awkward, and slightly depressing, when for instance I come out of Broadcasting House after doing a radio show such as *Loose Ends*, and I'm almost pushed over by a heaving throng of autograph hunters reaching over my shoulder desperately waving their pens at Diana Rigg.

It's also why there's nothing more flattering than being invited to something you would never take part in on principle. For example I'm extremely proud of an invitation I received to be in the audience for *An Audience With Jimmy Tarbuck*. Tarbuck is the latest in a line of talentless old buffoons who saw the way the wind is blowing towards comedians like Eddie Izzard and Jo Brand. These types of performers, far more inventive than he could ever wish to be, are attracting a mainstream audience the likes of Tarbuck must tap into if they're to remain stars.

So Tarbuck, Jim Bowen and Co are desperately trying to reinvent themselves into a kitsch image of classic old boys from the '70s by surrounding themselves with the younger comics. The only stand to take was not to go. But on the other hand I'd have been well fucked off if someone I knew had got an invitation and I hadn't.

The Slightly Successful Comedian understands that a comic's real ambition should be to wish to be funny by being passionate about things you love and vitriolic about things you hate, and that to convey that to a small number means far more than presenting *Lucky Numbers* to a large number.

But if you are half satisfied with something you've written or performed in, you must want it to go out to as many people as possible. In other words be more famous. And more successful. The egomaniac wants fame no matter how it comes.

The Slightly Successful Comedian craves respectability and fame. That's real megalomania.

At this point the person who said: 'Well, who knows. One day you might be famous,' will probably be saying: 'All right mate, I was only being polite.'

"And if Thy Right Eye Offend thee, pluck it out, AND CAST it FROM Thee ..."

'He's like a cross between Steven Wright and Woody Allen – only not as funny as either of them.'

25
Richard Bucknall

....tells about his career as an 'Agent Provocateur'

My first signing were The Insinuendos. They were a four man song and dance act who specialised in rewriting the lyrics of composers like Cole Porter. I met them one dark winter's night in a tower block in Kennington. For about an hour they explained what they did, and I explained how I could help them do it (improvisational skills helped here). Two days later they called and said I could start in January.

Lesson One: always go and see an act before you agree to represent them. It's January 5th and I'm in the council chamber at Islington Town Hall, watching The Insinuendos and The Pink Singers perform in front of The Mayor. Watching three guys dressed in pink tutus singing *Que Sera Sera* makes me realise that I can look at the situation in one of two ways: I can either think 'how can I get out of this?' or I can think 'what can I do with them?' I chose the latter and my fate is sealed.

Seven years later, I work out of an office in Covent Garden with a client list of twelve brilliant comedians, and a highly efficient assistant called Caroline.

I had become an agent via actor-touring in an old transit van, playing three different parts in panto, operating the lights and sound, and driving (all for seventy quid a week), radio work, more touring, theatre-entertainment in old people's homes, car jockey for the Chicago Ribshack, door-to-door sales-man, selling roofs and cavity wall insulation. One time I was interviewed for a job as a pebble-dash salesman. The guy showed me pictures of the product and asked me what I thought. Not my cup of tea, I said... well it was more like 'rub-bish' actually. However, the point of the story is that as far as he was concerned, people can't sell things they don't like. I thought you could. But not any more. I represent people I like and who have the potential to do really well. My thanks go out to that pebble-dash guy, he taught me a salutary lesson.

Live theatre has held me in its grip since the age of six, when my grandmother took us to see *Toad of Toad Hall*. I was entranced. But what really gripped me was what was going on behind the scenes. From then on, I seized upon every opportu-nity to be involved in the theatre. At school I directed a Noel Coward play. Having assembled some 1920s props, including a wind-up gramophone I neglected to consider the furniture, and sitting right on centre stage were two armchairs and a sofa that could have been used for a backdrop in a Brian Ferry video, circa 1976. I felt marginally better when the audience applaud-ed as the curtain went up.

Back to 1987: I had my first act and I had to find them work. The first gig I booked was at The Exeter and Devon Arts Centre. This genteel town is situated in one of the most conser-vative (with a big 'C', too) areas in the country. Even so, I was surprised to receive a phone call the day before the gig from the Centre's director, informing me that some interest had been shown by the local press. Some interest! The headline that day read: 'Gay act comes to Exeter... AIDS scare'. A local vicar had written in to the paper calling homosexuals 'divine abominations'. Great, I thought, we can use that on the poster. As soon as I put down the phone, it rang again; this time it was BBC Radio Exeter asking for a comment. I commented quite succinctly. After the initial disappointment of not getting a press reception at the station, the boys left to thunderous applause and glowing reviews.

Having forgotten my initial misgivings, I was now convinced this was a great act: good voices, good movers and above all, they possessed an unshakeable belief in their own abilities. They were The Goods. It was my job to push them forward. I booked them into The Gilded Balloon for a three week run at the Edinburgh Fringe. As one of the Insinuendos' numbers was a safe sex song, I approached The London Rubber Company for sponsorship. They politely declined due - they said – to the humour factor, which is like the X-factor but funnier. In the end we had to make do with three ice cream trays from Walls, and they threw condoms out of these at the beginning of each show.

Accommodation in Edinburgh at Festival time is at a premium, but I thought that 'three bedrooms' meant what it said, and not one bedroom with twin beds and a kitchen diner. I had three very angry people on my hands, but luckily a friend of a friend of a friend helped out, and they stayed in luxury at Morningside. The income from that three weeks was not huge, but it was bolstered by sales of their cassette, *Live at the Gate, Notting Hill*.

The following year we parted company; partly because I wanted to go to America for a while, and partly because the politics of a group had become difficult. I was grateful to The Insinuendos for giving me a break, and therefore the memories are good. My only sadness is that Vaughan and Gered have both since died, a great loss.

In the meantime I had signed several other acts, including The Crisis Twins and Sean Hughes. It was through The

Crisis Twins that I met Sean, because I was at the Watermans Arts Centre to see them perform. Sean had just arrived from Ireland and was putting himself around the circuit. His act was then, as it is now, a completely original view of the world, but in those days it was a stream of one-liners.

'What do you want to do?' I asked him.

'Write and make films,' he replied.

Two weeks later we met in a pub on the Charing Cross Road, and I became his agent. The first television deal I did for Sean was for *Friday Night Live*, which at the time was a must for all comics to appear on.

Shortly afterwards I took a trip to the States, partly for a holiday, and partly to have a look at the comedy scene over there. It was exploding. There were clubs in every city, and new networks such as the Comedy Network produced stand up and sit -com shows. Whilst I was excited by the growth, I was also depressed by the sameness of it all. There were exceptions like Bill Hicks, Will Durst, Steven Wright and more recently Harland Williams (Canadian), but there seemed to be a tendency to whoop the crowd up, and then leave them twenty minutes later.

In Boston I met Bill Downes of The Comedy Connection and persuaded him to book Sean for a two week run at his main club, and at others in the region. After a false start involving no work papers (so no tour), and a resulting flight to Boston to file for temporary papers, the tour finally happened. Not surprisingly, Sean was slightly aghast when faced with the venue on the opening night of the tour. It was a beer hall in the suburbs, with a comic who asked if he worked clean or dirty, to which Sean replied that he just stuck to the jokes.

After that, the tour improved and Sean performed three storming nights at The Connection, followed by dates all around New England. Since then the American comedy industry has gone through a recession, clubs have closed and work for a lot of comics has been hard to find. A lot of people went into the business believing comedy equals money, and expecting to become millionaires overnight. Many of them have been burnt. It is an important lesson to learn. I take the long term view and believe that you have to nurture acts before they can start to break through. The important thing for them is to do as much live work as possible, and the TV will follow naturally.

I came back and was offered a job at Sharon Hamper's agency. I brought in Sean Hughes, Johnny Immaterial (now Meres), and Donna McPhail. We booked tours for them around the country under the title *The Big Coat Show* (why?!!?), and got them a three night residency at The Riverside Studios. The show broke even on the guarantee, which at the time was quite an event.

Soon afterwards, Sean won the Perrier Award and was commissioned to write *Sean's Show* for Channel 4. The phone was red hot with independent production companies ringing up, all dying to produce it. We went with Channel X and did two series. In the meantime, feeling an itch to work for myself, I set up RBM in an alcove, with just enough room for a typewriter, a filing cabinet and one phone.

The first new signing for the agency was John Shuttleworth (Graham Fellows). I first saw him at a Sunday night at The Chuckle Club and there were about ten people in the audience. An oldish man with specs sauntered on to the stage and spoke with a soft Yorkshire accent. I was in stitches for the next twenty minutes. I have never acted so fast.

'That was great, I want to represent you.' I told him straight afterwards.

It was a struggle to start with, but within a year John Shuttleworth had a Perrier Nomination, a radio pilot under the belt of his imitation leather jacket and a regular appearance on Channel Four's *Saturday Zoo*.

The stiltwalker still makes me laugh. l saw him in Carnaby street wearing aviator sunglasses and a flying jacket terrorising passers by. We booked him in to all the rave parties – the crowds loved it. Then he disappeared for a year, next time I saw him was at The Edinburgh Festival and we arranged to meet for a drink the following day. He didn't turn up – no surprise – but when I got back to the flat, I discovered a message to say he'd been hospitalised. He'd walked in to an over -head fan in a nightclub. The last time I heard of him was at a wine festival in Bremen, it was the last booking I got him and he still owes me £250.00. Reward paid!

The first time I booked The Bloomsbury Theatre for Shuttleworth, I was nervous. But we did fine, I went back six months later for two nights, and we barely scraped by; but a year later we were there for three nights and had capacity crowds. Bruce Morton has a tough time in London, but in Scotland he sells out everywhere. Next time he comes back down I'm sure he'll do brilliantly. It's tough for me when there's a low crowd, or the show's not cooking. But, it's even tougher for them. I think you have to be unreasonable to do what the comic does, and when I'm in the middle of a deal and the other party is complaining about our 'unreasonable and outrageous demands' it doesn't faze me, because I know that they're going to realise at the end of the job that the price was worth paying.

I think back to The Insinuendos and we're in a field in Essex. It's a Greenpeace event, and the piano from the local church is out of tune, and we move to a smaller tent, and the kids are running around with fire torches, and there's a howling gale outside, and meanwhile I'm being paid the fee in a caravan in small change, and eventually we disappear into the night minus three tap shoes and a tutu.

It's all a bit of a laugh, isn't it?

26

Bruce Dessau

...writing about 'Writing About Comedy'

Who said that writing about music was like dancing about architecture? Whoever it was had obviously never attempted to write about comedy, which must be like ice-skating about Monopoly. I've spent more than five years attempting to come up with the perfect piece of prose about the subject and while I've made a healthy living out of it, I doubt if I've actually written anything that I've been completely satisfied with.

The problems begin at the beginning and end at the end. I've conducted interviews which have gone along swimmingly, witty banter being exchanged like some latter-day recreation of Dorothy Parker and Co at the Algonquin, only for the tape to be mangled or my notes to be savaged by a passing pit bull terrier. But that could happen to any journalist writing about any subject. Comedy has its own inherent problems. It's like the old gag about the football team who are brilliant on paper but crap on grass. What's funny on tape is never quite the same on the newsagent's shelf.

A pretty handy axiom of hacks is 'if in doubt, blame the editor'. Why is it that when they send me out to interview a comedian they want the feature to be funny? If they were packing me off to interview a poet they wouldn't want it to rhyme.

Or if they were commissioning me to write about medicine they wouldn't want the piece to cure their piles.

There's this idea that writing about, say, a stand-up club comedian should recreate the mood of his act so that readers enjoy the article and then decide to pay money to see the act. In a lot of senses, writing about a comedian is closest of all to writing for a pornographic magazine – you are expected to arouse, excite and make the reader want to be intimately involved with your subject. Or so a friend of a friend of someone I met in the pub tells me.

If you approach your task with a scientific rigor worthy of NASA this can result in a successful mission. When I interviewed David Baddiel and Frank Skinner last year to coincide with their new series of *Fantasy Football League*, I took along a prepared tape of football songs for them to identity. Things didn't look promising in advance – the interview was scheduled for a day when they were based in an alien hotel room and would have numerous journalists trooping in and out, but the freshness of the idea, plus the added bung of showing Frank Skinner a rare copy of Derek Dougan's only novel, seemed to do the trick. Baddiel waxed lyrical about his girlfriend meeting the U2 guitarist and thinking the Edge was called Reg. Skinner regaled me with the incredible tale of West Bromwich's Jeff Astle – who couldn't carry a tune if it was placed in a bag and handed to him – getting a recording contract after the number one success of the England World Cup Squad's *Back Home* in 1970. The interview sounded good, it read well, and I'd like to take some credit for the fact that when the series re-appeared Jeff Astle had been invited to close each show with some of the worst renditions of some of your favourite songs you are ever likely to be confronted with. Then again, apart from the advance preparation, my input was minimal in the writing of the piece. All I did was type out their words.

The secret is clearly in the planning. An interview with Harry Enfield's regular TV accomplice Paul Whitehouse was scheduled to coincide with the release of Robert Altman's fashion film *Prêt-à-Porter*. I faxed Whitehouse with this information first and asked him to think about what his smutty tailor character Suit You would have to say about fashion; when we spoke later in the week I got a radiant interview and Paul Whitehouse told me that he had got a radiant idea for a Suit You sketch measuring supermodels' inside legs for his next series of *The Fast Show*.

Jack Dee, on the other hand, seemed to have an unusual attitude to press interviews. He also told me that he doesn't read them, so I can happily reveal here that he is a cantankerous old bugger with the dress sense of Lennie Peters of Peters and Lee; unless he lies to interviewers, in which case he is a lovely man with a lovely tailor. Interestingly, Dee told me that when he is booked to appear on something like Des O'Connor's chat show he will prepare new material in advance, comparing that aspect of chat to be akin to doing a stand-up spot. On the other hand, when I interviewed him we talked about his family, the problems of buying a house, and his manager. I learned a lot about home births, surveyors and how to earn the most money from corporate entertaining, but when it came to writing my usual deep, penetrating, pantaloon-pissingly funny feature it wasn't quite as productive.

Dee is a great comic with a classic, timeless style, but it still helps if you have his voice in your head when you read his gags on the page. Take: 'You'll have to excuse me if I seem a little tired. It was my wife's birthday yesterday and I got in at 4am. She was livid.' Put that one simple joke on paper and how do you convey the pauses, the ebbs and flows, the emphasis? How do you avoid taking it out of context and making Dee sound like a horrible old chauvinist? On film, you can do all sorts of things, on paper, using italics is virtually the only way to convey the gossamer-thin nuances of language. The only answer is that you know who Dee is and as you read it you imagine him saying it. But what if the gag is by Alan Davies? He is brilliantly funny, but when I interviewed him he had done little TV and was barely known outside London. As a result, if the same gag were to appear in an article about Davies and you didn't know him, would you think the gag, and *ipso facto*, Davies, was funny at all? At the best of times, funny live gags, and even more so, funny spontaneous ad-libs have a habit of wriggling loose and escaping when you try and trap them on the page. Spike Milligan is always telling people that he is a great ad-libber: 'I ad libber for breakfast this morning'. With a linguistically clever line like that, you can forget about raising a laugh, it's an achievement if the reader realises it's a joke and not a typographical error. Particularly when sub-editors get their hands on your copy. There's an only slightly apocryphal story about a sub-editor on *The Guardian* who read the pun 'Vorsprung Dirge Technik' in a piece about the lyrics of Blur's *Parklife* song and incorrectly corrected it to 'Vorsprung Durch Technik'.

Similarly, take a sketch which revolves around the crossed purposes which can occur when one of the characters gets the words 'salary' and 'celery' mixed up. The English language is tailor-made for spoken humour. Writing about spoken humour is a different stick of vegetable altogether. The title of this book says it all. Talk can be funny, the written word is something rather different. And these are the difficulties you encounter when you are dealing with essentially verbal entertainers. I have so far resisted the urge to interview Marcel Marceau, or confront any jugglers or acrobats – although the latter might make a nice balanced piece – but then Vic Reeves and Bob Mortimer are hard enough.

You start by meeting Bob and Vic in the pub, you chat about football and your favourite meats. It can all be very funny, but the moment you turn the tape recorder on, some of the magic flies out of the door. Vic can be shy and awkward, Bob can be suddenly serious, and the two blokes who have had you in stitches, not just on the box when they working from a script, but at the bar when they are off the cuff (a phrase that originated in the music halls when old comics used to write their routines on their cuffs) seem more like well-dressed slightly silly parents than an all-conquering comedy double act.

The Reeves and Mortimer chestnut is conclusive proof that the comedy-journalism interface is a strange and clumsy beast. In music journalism there's the cliché of the up-and-coming band claiming that they are making music because they like to, and if they sell lots of records then, *hey!* that's a bonus. In all my years as a comedy critic I've never encountered anyone who has said that they only make jokes because they like to, and, *hey!* if people laugh, or if they get a series on BBC1 then that's a bonus. Comedians tend to be more mature, more cynical and more ambitious than musicians; it's a lot easier for anyone to get up on stage and try their hand at comedy than it is to form a band, rehearse some songs, beg, steal and borrow some instruments and get a gig, yet by the time a comic is good enough to be interviewed by the press they know that means they are on their way to making it at least as far as television exposure. Perhaps it is because they see a press interview as the next stage on the way to global domination that they tend to take it so seriously and make my job so bloody hard.

Reeves and Mortimer must have known they were going to be stars back in 1987 when they hadn't really done any TV together (though Reeves had appeared a few times on *The Tube* when he was a Newcastle-area solo act in the early '80s) and were selling out in advance every Sunday night at Deptford's Albany Empire. They are amiable, helpful interviewees rather than ruthless, backstabbing careerists and yet conveying their on-stage nuttiness in the press has been an unenviable task. If you gave a monkey a typewriter and the rest of eternity he wouldn't be able to convey half the genius of Reeves and Mortimer. It's for this reason that despite being one of the comedy discoveries of the '80s, as well as personal favourites, I have frequently turned down the chance to write about them. Does that make me a coward, unable to accept a personal challenge? Or does that make me a realist, able to acknowledge the fundamental conundrum of writing about two grown men who can reduce fans to hysteria by waving a long stick, but who have yet to be captured on the page? When TS Eliot wrote in the *Four Quartets* that words 'slip, crack and break under the strain', he must have been trying to review an edition of *The Smell Of Reeves And Mortimer*.

There is a way out of this, of course. Let the artists speak for themselves, which is what a lot of this book does. That way they stand or fall on their own abilities. In journalism there is a tendency to shoot the messenger. In writing about comedy it is even worse than that. Just because all the words are in the dictionary there's more to this lark than rearranging them in the right order. If an article is not very good, you shoot the messenger after kicking him in the bollocks and shoving a custard pie in his face. If, by some bizarre fluke, the piece is hilarious, the reader's usual response is to say what a wise and witty fellow that Harry Hill/Alexei Sayle/Dawn French/ Robert Newman is, rather than praise the writer. I'm surrounded by people who read bylines, but then one of the occupational hazards of my field is that I am surrounded by pecking order-obsessed, greasy pole-climbing hacks who can't wait to find out who is getting the most column inches. Real people, on the other hand, only read the articles.

Which, I ought to conclude, is the one saving grace of this job. Well maybe not quite the only one. I get into comedy shows without paying, I earn a decent celery, I can rub shoulders with and spill the pints of some of the funniest people in the country. The problem is having to write about them after-wards. Still I suppose at the end of the day I just write for the sheer fun of it. If people like my work, then, *hey!* that's a bonus. And if you believe that you'll believe that Bernard Manning is doing a gig this week to raise money for Left Wing Lesbians at the Hackney Empire.

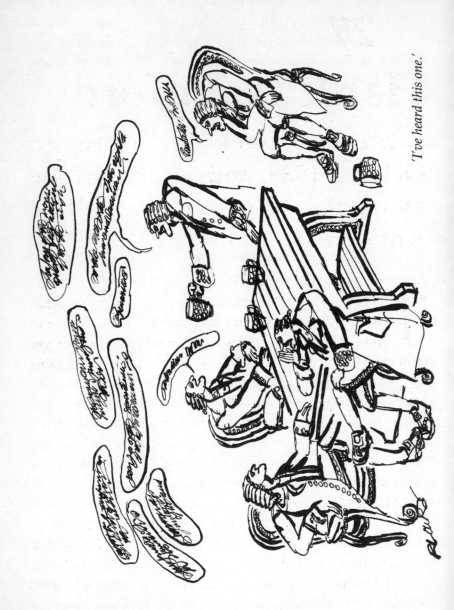

'I've heard this one.'

27
Hank Wangford

...travels back in time to October 1989, and – in Nashville at least – 'Gorbachov Is The Antichrist'

There are more churches than bars in Nashvllle. That doesn't mean it's difficult to get a drink, it's just easier to gain redemption afterward. But religion doesn't get rammed down your throat in Nashville, the Buckle on the Bible Belt, it just seeps up your trouser leg and oozes round under your shirt. It sticks to you. It hangs thick in the air. You find yourself praising the Lord for getting a cheque cashed or finding the right pair of Reeboks in Hickory Hollow Mall. This isn't trivialising God or sanctifying shopping, it's just that God Is Everywhere, even in a pair of Reeboks. There are Chapels in many of the Malls. First Church of Christ, Shopper.

It's all very intense and all very literal. God has to be everywhere because so is... Satan. The battle rages all around us, our faith in the Lord only just holding back Satan who is waiting to pounce at any moment. *Satan Is Real* sang the Louvin Brothers thirty years ago, not a *Concept* but *Flesh and Blood*. So the battle between God and the Devil will go on forever. Except perhaps in the empty, dead eyes of Jerry Lee Lewis where it looks like God has given up and gone home.

This Holy Battle has been chronicled for two hundred years now in the Athens of the South, and religious publishing still earns more than Nashville's two other stalwarts, Insurance and the Music Business. More money in Bibles than Bluegrass... The Dollar and the Cross were symbols of Nashville long before guitars came along. And the good folks are still praying all the way to the bank. *Insured Beyond The Grave* sang the Louvin Brothers.

20th Century Christian Parking was the best parking lot in town. We parked in there from time to time, but could never find the car park attendant to tell him we were Satanists and see if twenty dollars would let us stay. Would he be unbribable, a Godsworth? *Sorry, can't park that thing here, it's more than my God'sworth...* If things got rough I was ready to flash him my Bankon Christcard, a sacred plastic credit card I'd found in a God shop. 'Charge Your Life To Christ' it says, and 'Good thru – eternity'.

Just as well blessings don't have a use-by date.

God works in wondrous ways. None more wondrous than on TV where God has His own cable channel. Sadly, it isn't on for twenty-four hours, and stops at midnight. So at three in the morning, a lonely and troubled time, the Christian Channel is a fog of swirling white dots. God leaves Nashville in the night like Infinity's Policeman, never there when you most need Him.

The TV ministers have no fear. 'Satan Is Always There', warns Ernest Aingley, an Elmer Gantry hellfire preacher from way back, 'even when you Christian folk are on your way to Church on Sunday morning with your family, don't think you're safe because Satan is hiding behind that bush you're passing, just WAITING TO JUMP OUT AND GRAB YOU WHEN YOU'RE NOT LOOKING!'

We all know of the grown men weeping on screen as

they ask for money, for 'love gifts, tithes or offerings' to save their ministry. We've seen Jimmy Lee Swaggart, Jerry Lee Lewis's cousin, crying real tears asking his wife, his ministry and God forgiveness for playing Safe-Sex Doctors and Nurses with a hooker. We don't understand how they can take him back to their hearts, way the Americans love nothing more than a Sincere Sinner. We wonder how people can be foolish enough to send money to such obvious con artists. Well, it's just too easy for us smartass Brits to lean back on all our heritage and get patronising about the poor dumb Rednecks, sure they all have their names on the back of their cowboy belts so that when they take their heads out of their arses they'll know who they are. And it's too easy to get sanctimonious about the TV holy men with their hands in the till or their pants round their ankles.

Pat Boone, a squeaky-clean singer from the early Rock era with the feel of a young Val Doonican, is Born Again and a friend of Jimmy Swaggart. He won't defend the sinning but explains how it is that Jimmy can come back and take up his ministry again. If the Lord calls Jimmy to work for him, then He is following a pattern. There's only ever been one Perfect Being. All others have flaws, are *cracked vessels*. Look at the Bible. Abraham was a liar, denying his wife. Moses a murderer, hiding away for forty years. Paul was 'an informer, a Gestapo, a KGB kinda guy'. So if God could cope with Swaggart so could we. Pat got into his stride and wrote a song called *The Fallen Giant Will Rise Again*. It wasn't Country, more a pop song, with a 'sorta Miami Vice kind of feel'. And now Swaggart has come back to his ministry to build up his congregation again. Pat says his ratings had suffered *'grievous slippage'*.

Early one morning a quiet, reasonable man in a grey suit – not one of the more psychotic preachers or Pentecostal ravers – without a single tear in his eye, told us on TV why GORBACHOV IS THE ANTICHRIST. It was quite obvious, he said, that Gorby fulfilled fourteen of the sixteen criteria for being being the Antichrist. Lobster on his forehead, mark of the Beast, right. Antichrist. Such a nice guy, so charming? There you go again, the Antichrist. The Bible says he's going to be all of that, seductive, convincing, a blue-eyed boy. Finally be played his trump card: what about the Warsaw Pact countries? How many? Seven? Right, can't you see it? — the *Seven Headed Beast of the Apocalypse*! The rest of the proof was in his book *Gorbachov Is The Antichrist* which he'd happily send you free in exchange for a fifteen dollar love gift.

But this reasonable man's arguments, and many of America's foreign policies, are based on the crazed hallucinations of John the Mushroom-Eater in Revelations. The Beasts, the Boils and the Seas of Blood... The fiery star Wormwood, that fell to the ground poisoning the rivers and the seas, whose name in Russian is... *CHERNOBYL!* Aaargh! And the Fundamentalists won't go away. If they can have a group of TV Evangelists called the *Executive Board of Committee for the American Coalition for Traditional Values* answering to the President, we should still worry. Having God on your side is always the best justification for the worst action.

So I clutch my plastic Bankon Christcard close to my heart; like that cockroach it will survive the Holocaust and stay with my charred remains forever.

That was my impression of Nashville in 1989. Gorbachov has gone, and Nashville wants to call Country 'New American Music'. Otherwise, nothing has changed. – HW.

'Bye, bye, Miss American Pie!'

If you enjoyed

Funny Talk

you'll really enjoy

Rock Talk

'Rock Talk' features the very best of today's new rock 'n' roll writing. Twenty four musicians, artists, writers and broadcasters – many new to the written word – have taken the opportunity to explore subjects dear to their hearts. **Miles Hunt** – ex-**Wonder Stuff** – and **Chris Jagger** take us on tour with them, **Daevid Allen** explores the roots of **Gong**, **Nick Coleman** reflects on writing about music, and **Jon Ronson** whisks us off to the pop awards. **Roy Harper** looks back on a charmed life, **Tom Robinson** gives some advice, and there's a new poem (and more) from **John Cooper Clarke.Vince Power** recalls the trials and tribulations of setting-up his Mean Fiddler empire, **John Otway** explains how failure finally made him a success, *Time Out* music editor **Laura Lee Davies** writes on **Madness**, and **Doc Cox** reveals his darkest secret: **Ivor Biggun**. New fiction from **John B Spencer, Ron Kavana, Martin Roach** and **Darren Brown** (aka **Wiz** from **Mega City Four**) joins fine new writing by **Glen Colson, Laura Connelly, Wilko Johnson, Bruce Iglauer, Keith Bailey**, GLR's **Mary Costello** and **Jim Driver**.
Cover illustration and cartoons by **Ray Lowry**. (192 pp paperback)

ISBN 1 899344 00 4 Price £5.99

Available from good bookshops – or in case of difficulty
(£5.99, post free) from:
The Do-Not Press
PO Box 4215
London
SE23 2QD

Coming soon from The Do-Not Press…

Quake City

the long-awaited new Charley Case novel by

John B Spencer

The third in the acclaimed series in which science
fiction and crime *noir* collide. The streets of LA don't
come any meaner than after The Big One of '97…

To be published in November 1995 by The Do-Not Press.
ISBN 1 899344 02 0

If you have any comment to make, require more information, or
would like to be put on our mailing-list in order to receive advance
information on all future Do-Not Press publications, please send
your name and address to:

The Do-Not Press
PO Box 4215
London
SE23 2QD

JONGLEURS
COMEDY CLUBS

JONGLEURS: BYWORD FOR COMIC EXCELLENCE.

LAUGH, EAT, DANCE, LAUGH, DRINK

JONGLEURS HAS BEEN THE EARLY TESTING
GROUND FOR MANY HOUSEHOLD NAMES SUCH AS
FRY AND LAURIE, LENNY HENRY, RORY BREMNER,
BEN ELTON AND RUBY WAX.
IT REMAINS FOREMOST IN THE COMEDY WORLD
FOR A FULL EVENINGS ENTERTAINMENT.

BATTERSEA
49 LAVENDER GARDENS
BATTERSEA
LONDON
SW11

CAMDEN
MIDDLE YARD
CAMDEN LOCK
LONDON
NW1

ONE SHOW FRIDAY & TWO SHOWS SATURDAY
TICKETS AVAILABLE FROM THE JONGLEURS BOX
OFFICE ON:

0171 924 2766

TUESDAY TO SATURDAY, 12NOON-4PM.